SUNDOWN

SUNDOWN

A Western Duo

Lewis B. Patten

Five Star • Waterville, Maine

First Edition
First Printing: June 2005

Published in 2005 in conjunction with
Golden West Literary Agency.

Set in 11 pt. Plantin by Elena Picard.

Printed in the United States on permanent paper.

Library of Congress Control Number: 2005921813
ISBN 1-59414-133-9 (hc : alk. paper)

SUNDOWN

Table of Contents

Texas Maverick

I

Cold rain slanted out of the dark north sky, this night of Thomas Cady's homecoming. It dripped monotonously from the black brim of his cavalry hat onto his frayed and ancient rain cape that was waterproofed with gutta-percha. From there it ran into his saddle and onto his gray-clad knees, so that he wondered with mild ill humor if keeping a man's chest dry was worth the discomfort of having his seat perpetually wet like that of any untrained kid.

This was southern Texas, into which hundreds of defeated Confederate troops were filtering, heading for home. This was a choked, nearly impenetrable land of brush called the Big Thicket, lying south of Austin and north of the Gulf along the sluggish length of the Colorado River. Some of them came back, sullen and silent. Some were openly defiant. Yet all were alike in one respect—they were not truly defeated. The defeat was but a thing of paper treaty and of Army generals who had signed it. It was not a thing of the heart—not among these men, whose liberty and independence was a jealously guarded tradition.

A part of Tom Cady protested the rain and cold, yet another part of him reveled in it, for nothing brings out the smells of a place like falling rain—and smells are the things a man remembers when he's far away: the smell of wet mesquite, the smell of soaked and steaming ground. A horse has a wet smell and so does a man's clothing. As Tom re-

11

membered the old days, the harsh lines of his face relaxed.

A tall young man was Cady, twenty-two his last birthday. He looked older than that, for his body was gaunted by hunger and weariness, his face marked by a hundred cold nights under superior enemy fire. His eyes were aged by the sight of too much suffering and too much death, disillusioned and tired, but not yet turned bitter. The war was over, and tonight he was coming home.

Home to what? His mouth thinned out and his eyes held quiet, deep-hidden sadness and regret. His father was gone, dead these last two years. The shack in which they had lived had been claimed by the brush, and did not belong to Tom anyway, having been sold by the old man before he died. Home to a name, then, that folks distrusted because it had become synonymous with a wild and berserk fury they claimed could only have been insanity. Why then, Tom wondered, hadn't he turned around and ridden out of the country last night, right after he'd talked to Sheriff Durand in Matadero?

A good question, that. Tom rummaged in his mind for answers, remembering the blocky, grizzled Durand, the friendly smile that somehow had an edge to it like a sheathed razor.

"Hell of a homecoming, Tom," Durand had said, shaking that leonine head. "Your old man's dead. His place has been sold. The country's overrun with Union troops to back up all the vultures that have come in here from the North. I'd ride, boy. I'd get the hell out."

"If that's such good advice, why don't you follow it?"

The friendly smile had become less so. Durand had looked away and shrugged. "You know how it is. A man gets used to a place where he's spent his life. And sooner or later the bluebelly troops will leave."

12

"This is where I spent my life . . . except the last three years. I'm used to it, too. For now I'll stay."

Friendliness had remained on the sheriff's face, friendliness that had become a thing of expression and not of the heart. This had puzzled Tom. Why should Durand want him to leave? And why had Tom been so emphatic about his intent to stay, when in his heart he had not been certain at all? Well, a man's memories are hard to discard. If the memories are happy ones, he is loyal to them and to the places and people that gave them birth. Or maybe it had been only stubbornness.

They said Matt Cady had died in the plaza at Matadero. They said that out of a simple fight grew Matt's insane, murderous fury that scattered those who had tried to bring him down and left five of them dead and half a dozen wounded before they could succeed. But what had been the cause of Matt's sudden fury? That was a question for which they had no answers.

Rain slackened over the thicket, and then increased. Tom stayed on the road, as familiar to him as the back of his hand in spite of his long absence. Here was the turn-off that led to the Cady cabin, now almost overgrown with brush. Tom reined aside out of long-fixed habit, and halted, half uncertainly, while nostalgia touched him and vaguely softened the bleak contours of his face.

Almost angrily, afterward, he returned to the main road. For a while he rode swiftly, as though by so doing he could put his memories behind. Faintly, in distance, he heard the unmistakable *clatter* of a small patrol of cavalry, and quickly reined aside into the mesquite to wait. Leaning over, he clamped a big hand over the nostrils of his dripping mount. Habit, perhaps, or the ingrained caution of a man at war. Even here, avoidance of the military was wise. There were new laws in the land, laws every returning soldier heard about before he reached Texas, laws against the carrying of guns—even laws regulating the wearing of Confederate uniforms. Cady fingered the buttons of his coat, green now from corrosion. There were even laws against these, with penalties all out of proportion to the seriousness of the offense. You could wear the gray, but you had to replace the military buttons with civilian ones before you could. Then there was the matter of the cape, taken from the body of a dead Union officer and clearly Union property. So many new, regulatory laws that even the most law-abiding might be accused of violating one. Law had become a club, by which the military held the vanquished, bitter civilian in line.

The patrol went past, wordless and silent in their soggy misery, led by a civilian who in darkness looked like Sheriff Durand, and by an officer Tom had never seen. Again Tom Cady came out upon the road.

At midnight he heard the low bawling of cattle ahead, and shortly thereafter he came into a large clearing of sacahuista grass. A long, adobe building and a couple of large corrals contained half a dozen horses, standing hip-shot over the trampled remains of a few forkfuls of hay. The other contained cattle. Tom knew this was Schofield's headquarters.

The scraped-hide windows of the building were dark. With a sigh that reluctantly relinquished hopes of food and a dry bed, Cady turned his horse into the corral and found himself a place to sleep on the south side of the building and beneath its overhanging eaves. In an instant he was asleep and snoring softly. War taught a man to sleep instantly in spite of discomfort. It taught him to wake the same way, but at times weariness becomes too much.

★ ★ ★ ★ ★

It was silence that awakened Tom—silence following a normal noise of activity and men's voices that had, in itself, failed to arouse his exhausted senses. He opened his eyes, and at ground level saw the scuffed, worn boots of half a dozen men not a yard from his head. He turned his head and the sun blinded him. Shielding his eyes with a hand, he got to his feet and faced them, his back to the wall. "Mister Schofield around?" he asked, in a voice that croaked from the disuse of the night.

Something about the way they looked at him put him on his guard. As though they knew him.

Impatience touched him, but he kept his voice mild. "I asked if Mister Schofield was around."

It was there, and not imaginary. He could feel their hostility as tangibly as he could the adobe bricks of the wall at his back. He saw no familiar faces, but only strange and hostile ones.

One of them shouted: "Curt! Somebody here to see you!"

Tom waited, relaxed and easy, but puzzled, too.

He was not prepared for the size of the man who came around the corner of the building, but it was a deceptive size, for as the man came face to face with him, Tom realized he was no taller than Tom himself. The impression of size remained. Schofield's shoulders, wider than Tom's, hunched forward a little and gave Schofield the stooped and shambling appearance of a bear. Massive was the word for his body, from his monstrous depth of chest to his corded, knotty, and stocky legs, and it fitted his face as well. His forehead loomed, bony and high, above brows that suggested the spread wings of a golden eagle. His nose was broken and flattened, his mouth both thin and cruel. A

15

cropped and bristling beard hid his chin. He had the biggest ears Tom had ever seen on a man, although they lay flat and snug against his bony, close-cropped head. But his eyes seized and held Tom's attention. Tiny and close-set, they reminded Tom of the edgy, angry eyes of a wild boar.

Schofield's voice was the voice Tom expected to come from such a brute of a man, deep and barking, and without warmth: "What the hell do you want?"

Tom spoke as pleasantly as he could under the circumstances. "I want a job. I'm Tom Cady. I was raised around here and know the brush like I know the palm of my hand."

"Matt Cady's kid." Schofield made it a statement, not a question.

Tom nodded. His earlier impression of an angry boar did not decrease as a throbbing vein began to pulse on Schofield's forehead. He said: "You think I owe you a job because I bought your old man's place?"

Tom shook his head.

Schofield said: "That's good. Because I don't owe you a damn' thing. Now get out of here. Get off my land. I want no crazy wild Cadys on it."

Anger roused itself in Tom, but he fought it down determinedly. He shrugged. "All right. It's your land. But I've ridden all night. I could use a meal. I'll pay you for. . . ."

The vein in Schofield's forehead seemed about to burst. "You leave the country, boy, and don't come back." He took a step away from Tom, a wary step that served as a warning to his men.

The move puzzled Tom sorely. He could not believe that Schofield was afraid of him. Then it occurred to him that Schofield was trying to implant the suggestion among his men that, if old Matt had gone berserk, his son might, too.

He made himself grin, although the attempt was more of

a grimace than a smile. He said carefully: "All right. I'll get my horse."

He started across the yard toward the corral, but Schofield's hand caught him and swung him around by the frayed sleeve of his coat. He yanked free and the coat tore. Schofield's voice came rushing at him: "Wait a minute, you!"

Wildness surged and boiled in Tom, but still he held it checked. "What's the matter now?"

"Feed for the horse, Johnny Reb. It'll be a dollar."

Tom found it increasingly hard to speak evenly. "He didn't get any feed, and a dollar's four times too much even if he had. I turned him in at midnight and the hay was gone."

Schofield's face was bleak and without expression, but something in his eyes warned Tom he was being baited.

"A dollar," repeated Schofield implacably. "If you ain't got it, maybe I ought to take it out of your hide."

Tom settled more solidly on his feet. This man didn't mean to let him get away unless he crawled. Even crawling might not help. He stopped holding himself in. He said: "Why, mister, maybe you'd just better go ahead and try that. Could be you'll get even less hide than I got hay."

He expected some swiftness from Schofield, but not quite so much as the man showed. Schofield's huge hand shot out, gathered a fistful of Tom's coat front, and yanked. As Tom jerked forward, off balance, Schofield brought his knee up.

It would have been a crippling blow if Tom hadn't been expecting something of the kind. He turned his body like a dancer, bringing his knees up toward his chest. The maneuver threw his whole weight upon Schofield's grasp of his ragged coat. It tore and Tom fell away, but Schofield met the unexpected with all the grace of a cat. As Tom fell, Schofield dived forward at him, driving his knees at Tom's unprotected belly.

Tom rolled convulsively, and the big man's knees and weight took him in the side. Pain filled Tom's abdominal cavity like acid, and he felt the crack of breaking ribs. He gasped for air. His hands reached for Schofield's throat. Instead, they encountered the man's huge ears, and Tom seized one in each hand and twisted with all the strength he could muster.

Schofield's roar was like the infuriated bellow of a longhorn bull. His big hands closed over Tom's wrists and yanked Tom's hands away.

Tom tore them free and drove a smashing right into Schofield's unprotected mouth. He felt a solid urge of satisfaction as lips and teeth gave beneath its force.

I'll take it out of your hide! The words hung in Tom's mind, and grew, until he forgot all else. The strength in his body exploded like a charge of black powder, expending itself completely in the split part of a second. Schofield, for all his weight, was flung aside. Tom rolled. Once clear of the bigger man, he brought his hands and knees under him, then forced himself to his feet.

It was agony just to stand. With every breath, pain shot through Tom's body like a stabbing bayonet. But Schofield was coming again, shuffling along like an angered bear, spitting out blood and broken teeth.

Tom crouched slightly, then launched himself as Schofield came within range. He caught Schofield's nose with the heel of his right hand, coming up in a rising arc, and Schofield's head snapped back like the tip of a bullwhip. Tom followed through with his right elbow, bringing it slashing against Schofield's exposed throat.

Schofield went to his knees, gagging. His nose streamed blood, his eyes tears. Tom's breath came raggedly and in hoarse gasps. He panted: "You'll let me go now?"

He got no answer. Schofield struggled to his feet. He was hurt, but not hurt as Tom was, deeply, where it made a difference.

Schofield came on again, discarding the doubtful niceties of barroom brawling, wanting but one thing, to get Tom's body between his monstrous hands. Tom doubled his fist and with a certain desperation brought it up from knee level as he drove forward. It sank halfway to his wrist in Schofield's belly. That belly was not as soft as it looked, but it gave under the force of the blow. A wheezy grunt escaped the compressed lips and Schofield stopped as though he had run into a wall.

Suddenly Tom knew he must end this or be overwhelmed. He began to fight like a machine, expending his strength recklessly. He fought without thought, knowing only the burning need to destroy, to maim, to break once and for all. His fists drove out like locomotive pistons. They landed in Schofield's face, on his throat, on his chest and belly. They crowded back his grasping hands and tore loose when his hands fastened upon one or the other of Tom's wrists. They cut Schofield's face to ribbons, and tore open his eyebrows, hardly more than scar tissue anyway, thus releasing a flood of blood into his eyes.

Wounded and bewildered, Schofield stood in one spot, turning a little to meet Tom's charges, but giving not an inch of ground. And Tom knew, with a sense of defeat, that he had neither the strength nor the power to put the big man down and keep him there.

Tom's arms were lead now. His lungs were fire. A knife stabbed and twisted his side with each small movement. He choked out the words: "Got your money's worth yet?"

Schofield blinked. A huge paw came up to swipe away the blood. His little eyes emerged, red and swollen and almost closed. Fury blazed from them, fury as implacable as the yellow fire in a cougar's eyes.

The man's voice seemed to come from the very depths of his great, scarred body. "No! Get him, Ziegler!"

Too late, Tom whirled. A man dived at his legs, knocking them out from under him. As he fell, another struck his shoulder. As he hit the ground, a third fell across his legs, pinning them down to the ground, and a fourth jumped astride his chest.

Bony fists began to rain into Tom's unprotected face, and there was no escape. A boot crashed into the side of his head. Bright lights flashed in a growing darkness. Again the boot landed, and again.

But Tom's vision cleared for an instant before the haze of unconsciousness came down. He saw the man draw back his boot for another kick, and beheld his eyes that were hot and bright with cruel pleasure. Tom made a promise, somewhere in the back of his mind: *You'll pay for this. You'll pay, and Schofield will, and the price will be higher every day until you do.*

The kick landed, and Tom's head whirled and reeled from its force. A brackish, brassy taste invaded his mouth. Consciousness held for an instant more, an instant of the most terrible fury that Tom had ever known, an instant of berserk rage that demanded but one thing—the death of his tormenters. Was this the way his father had felt that day in Matadero's plaza? The thought came to Tom Cady, and then it was gone as blackness like night descended upon Tom Cady's world.

II

Consciousness came, and went, and came again, but only partially and with vague awareness of pain and movement. His head hung down, and blood congested in it, making it seem to be filled with a liquid under intense pressure. But gradually, as time went on, he understood that he was slung, belly down, across a horse's back and tied with his belt to the saddle horn. Thorns of the granjeno bushes had torn his neck and one side of his face. His hat was gone, his trouser legs in shreds.

He struggled, and waves of dizziness washed over his mind. He rested, and struggled again. Finally he got the reins and turned the horse, then gradually brought him to a halt. He could not force himself upright in the saddle because of the belt which was tied with rawhide to the saddle horn. But eventually he was able to work his hands under his belly and unfasten the buckle. He tried to ease himself upward into the saddle, but because he was heavier in chest and shoulders than in his legs, he fell forward and struck the ground on his head. He held to the reins grimly, although the horse fought and struggled to pull away. Tom was dragged a dozen feet before the horse would halt.

He made it to his knees before he rested again. He kept trying to remember what had happened to him, but memory was as elusive as a wisp of smoke on a windy day. From hands and knees he came to his haunches, and afterward struggled to his feet. He stood there, swaying, dizzy, fighting to retain his stance and the consciousness so recently returned but so eager to slip away.

How long he stood thus, he could not have said. But the time came when the dizziness began to pass away, and then he staggered to the horse's side and grasped the skirt of the saddle.

The simple act of mounting became an impossible task, one that must be considered owlishly and deliberately from all angles before he made the attempt. He tried to remember which foot went into the stirrup, and chuckled foolishly when memory refused to come. The details of mounting were like the elusive strains of a half-forgotten melody, near the surface of his mind, yet refusing to emerge in tangible form. But gradually, as he stood there struggling, anger began to rise, and with it came quickened heartbeat and renewed strength. He forced doubt from his mind, grabbed the saddle horn with both hands, slammed a foot into the stirrup, and swung astride.

The horse began to move at once. Tom sat for a few moments, swaying, fighting to retain the consciousness that his exertion now tried to steal away. He was hurt, sick. He needed help and food. His broken ribs needed tight bandages and a little rest. He cast around in his pain-wracked brain. Who had the Cadys' neighbors been? Tom frowned irritably, for he could remember none of their names. But suddenly one name took form. McGuire. Doc McGuire.

He reined aside automatically as he thought of Doc McGuire. In spite of pain and weakness, he chuckled softly to himself. You came home after an absence of three years and enemies cast you adrift in the trackless brush. Yet you knew where you were and which way you had to go to reach a certain place. He pondered the wonder of that directional sense. Was it born in a man, did those who lived in the thicket develop it out of sheer necessity?

His brain tired of activity before he arrived at any conclusion. He just rode, head slumped forward, body relaxed and limp in his saddle. Thorny branches of black chaparral clawed at his ragged coat. He avoided their raking on face and neck by an instinctive moving back and forth of his head.

He startled a family of wild pigs, and they scattered, squealing. A rattlesnake buzzed as he passed, but Tom scarcely heard, although his horse shied and afterward broke into a trot.

The sun sank behind the western horizon. The sky flamed orange, and pink, then faded to a deepening, soft gray. Dusk dropped down, and a yellow moon began to rise in the east. A wolf began to howl, and somewhere a longhorn bull bellowed a throaty challenge.

By moonlight, Tom came to the ponderous, three-storied house of Doc McGuire. It was wholly dark, save for faint lamplight that flickered from the kitchen windows. Tom caught a whiff of sour mash, which Doc no doubt fed to his hogs. He halted his horse at the clearing's edge and stared. The monstrous house never failed to evoke in him a feeling of incredulity. Unless you saw it, you wouldn't believe there could be such a thing here in the thicket. Columns that had once been white rose from the front verandah a full three stories to the roof. In moonlight the house possessed a grandeur always dispelled by daylight, for the soft light of the moon hid all deterioration and decay.

A half dozen hogs rooted idly, grunting softly near the back door. Doc sat on a bench beside the open door, his Mexican cigar making a bright, friendly spot of light.

Tom reined up and braced himself for the effort and pain of dismounting. He said: "Hello, Doc McGuire. It's Tom Cady."

Doc's voice was cracked and querulous. "Tom? Back from war?"

Tom said: "I'm back."

"Well, whadda ya know? Get down. And have a drink."

Tom clenched his teeth and slid from the saddle. He stood for a moment, clinging there and reluctant to leave until the reeling world quieted and steadied. Then he left the horse and walked, slowly and carefully, to where McGuire sat.

McGuire's head was a faceless blur. Tom took the proffered jug and put it to his mouth. He gagged on the raw whiskey, but he tried again and managed at last to swallow twice. The liquor turned his bruised mouth to flame. It built a fire in his stomach. Warmth from it began to course through his veins.

Doc turned and shouted reedily: "Hazel! Come see who's here!"

Tom remembered Hazel as a leggy, half-wild creature, more boy than girl, but a woman came to the door and stood silhouetted by its light. A woman's full-cadenced voice asked: "Who's here, Pa?"

"Tom Cady. He's home from the war."

Tom knew if he stayed out here much longer he was going to fall down. So he stepped across to the door and pushed his way inside.

Hazel stepped back. A gasp of frightened surprise escaped her lips. Tom grinned crookedly as he teetered and swayed in the doorway. She snatched a chair and shoved it under him. He sat down heavily and the chair creaked on its wobbly legs.

"What happened to you?" Hazel said in a shocked whisper.

"Schofield." The room began to swim before Tom's eyes. He heard Hazel's high cry: "Pa! Come here quick! He's hurt!" Then the room dissolved into whirling lights and he felt his face go forward and hit the floor.

Returning to consciousness was a gradual thing, similar to his earlier experience except this time there was no sensation of movement. He opened his eyes upon a world bright with sunlight, and found himself in a bed somewhere in the depths of the great house. His clothes were gone and his middle was tightly wound with strips of white cotton cloth. His face felt hot, and he hoped Doc and not Hazel had been the one to bandage him.

He heard steps creaking along the hall outside his room. A moment later, Hazel came in, carrying a steaming bowl of soup on a tray. This was not the Hazel that Tom remembered. He tried to recall how old she had been when he went away, and guessed she must have been about fourteen. That would make her seventeen or eighteen now.

Her face was still and almost cold. Her eyes held an odd expression that might have been either anger or dislike. She said: "Feel better?"

He nodded. "If you'll bring my clothes, I'll. . . ."

"Go out and get yourself half killed again?"

He struggled upright, wincing with pain in his ribs, hunching a little as pain began to pound in his head. She sat down indifferently beside the bed and held the tray while he awkwardly spooned the scalding soup into his mouth. He had the oddest impression that it pleased her to see him helpless, although he could not guess why.

He studied her face as he ate, and its beauty amazed him. Her hair was black, although not the blue-black of the Mexican women. In daylight, it had highlights that were almost gold. Her eyes were the green of the Gulf on a bright day, yet like the Gulf waters they held a threat of storm and violence. Except for a small bridge of pale freckles across her nose, her skin was white. Her body, even cased in its heavy dress, was strong and womanly and finely made.

She watched him moodily while he finished the soup, then took the tray and turned away. Tom let his eyes wander over the room. The walls were cracked and peeling. Great chunks of plaster had fallen from the water-stained ceiling, exposing the naked lath. Both bed and covers had a musty odor, as though they had been long stored away. Hazel's dress was of heavy brocade. Although it fitted her well, it was faded in stripes so that Tom knew it had been made from a pair of old draperies. She stood at the window, looking out.

Doc came in, unshaven, his eyes bloodshot and vague. "How you feel this mornin'?"

"Better, Doc. Where's my clothes?"

Hazel answered the question with curt unfriendliness. "I'll bring them."

She turned to go, almost as though she were angry. Doc looked at Tom apologetically. "Don't mind her," he said, and he sounded ashamed. "She ain't got much use for men. Those that come for whiskey sometimes get notions they can buy anything on the place. And I reckon I ain't nothing to make her proud."

Tom felt his bandages gingerly, embarrassed and anxious to change the subject. "How many ribs broken?"

"Three." Doc's eyes tried to focus on him. "What was the whippin' for, son?"

Tom shrugged, and immediately winced. "I don't know. He refused me a job. Refused even to feed me. Told me to get out of the country. As I was leaving, he tried to charge me a dollar for hay my horse never even got. I was edgy by then. I told him to take it out of my hide." He couldn't help a rueful grin. "He did a fair job of it, too."

Doc chuckled. "What are you going to do about it?"

Tom sobered. "I don't know. But I'm not going to leave." He remembered the raw fury that had coursed through him last night. He remembered, also, and reluctantly, the way Matt Cady had died. Could it be that folks were right? Did a streak of craziness run in Tom the way they said it had in Matt?

The fury he had felt yesterday was different from the emotions experienced by a man at war. You seldom got angry in battle. You just got scared, and, because you didn't want anyone to know, you went ahead, doing what you knew you had to do but not becoming personally involved in it. Yesterday had been different from that. There had been personal outrage in him yesterday exceeding anything he had ever felt before. Had he been able, he would have killed Schofield.

Hazel came back, carrying Tom's clothes, which had been washed and mended. She looked at him coldly, and again she left the room.

Tom swung his feet over the edge of the bed and sat up. His ribs gave him sharp pains, which were nothing, however, compared to those of last night. With some difficulty he slipped into his clothes and pulled on his boots. He stood up and his senses reeled. He steadied himself on the doorjamb.

"What are you going to do now?" Doc McGuire asked.

Tom shrugged. "Hides fetch a good price at Indianola. Maybe I'll skin a few steers."

"Schofield ain't going to like it."

Tom scarcely heard McGuire's words. He remembered his vengeful promise to the man who had kicked him in the head, and to Schofield. He frowned, puzzled by Schofield's senseless antagonism. He said: "I've been told to leave

27

twice now, by Durand in Matadero, and by Schofield."

"You going to leave?"

"Not until I know why they want me to."

McGuire looked at him sharply. He seemed anything but vague now. It was almost as though an idea had suddenly been born in the old man's mind. He said: "Stay here a week or two, at least until those ribs knit some. Don't let Hazel run you off."

After that, the old man turned hastily away. Tom followed him down the creaking stairs, avoiding the tread that was missing, and walked down a wide hall to the kitchen. Tom could remember this house when it had been the showplace of the countryside. Those days, there had been a lawn in front, and the shrubs had been carefully tended. Three Negroes had tended to Doc McGuire's wants and those of his wife.

Then Doc's wife had died, leaving him with Hazel, a baby. And Doc had begun to drink. Gradually the house had gone to ruin. Mesquite had invaded the lawn and grounds. The Negroes had run away, and Doc didn't even try to get them back. Gradually Doc's money had disappeared. Because he had to live, because no one would trust him to doctor them, he had built himself a still somewhere out in the brush.

Now he made whiskey and sold it in stoneware jugs. Unshaven, untidy, he sat all day on the bench beside the kitchen door, chewed tobacco, and drank occasionally from a jug.

McGuire went outside, but Tom halted in the kitchen. He looked at Hazel, fully aware of both her beauty and her coldness. He said: "Thanks for taking such good care of me. I'm not likely to forget it."

She didn't reply.

Tom said, bitterly sarcastic: "This is a nice, friendly country, full of nice, friendly people. Maybe I ought to leave, after all."

Her face flushed. "Nobody asked you to stagger in here last night."

"No, you didn't, did you? Schofield didn't ask me to visit his place, either. What's the matter with you . . . both of you? What are you afraid of?"

She flared up with an intensity that surprised him. "I don't know about Schofield. But look around you. Look at this house. Look at my father. I'm scared, and I admit it. Someday he'll ride off into the brush and won't come back. Then what do I do? Take up where he left off? Do you think I want to run a roadhouse out here in the thicket?"

Tom said quietly: "Women have been known to get married."

She laughed harshly. "That's not what they offer me! And if I did get married, would I be any better off, living in a tarpaper shack and raising a dozen kids that are hungry and cold half the time?" She halted, trembling and white-faced. She held out her hands piteously and her voice was a cry. "Where's the dignity of living, Tom? Where can I find it?"

"I don't know," Tom said. He felt hopeless and inadequate, but he understood her coldness now. He wanted to cross the room and take her in his arms. She was like a child, frightened and angry, but she was a woman, too, filled with emotion both wild and utterly honest.

Outside, a horse pounded away through the brush. Tom looked at Hazel questioningly.

"It's only Pa," she said wearily. "He's always riding off into the brush somewhere. But he'll be back for supper."

She sat down and smoothed her skirt with nervous

hands. She managed a rueful, tremulous smile. "I'm sorry."

Tom said: "Forget it." He grinned at her reassuringly, then went on out the door.

He found his horse in the corral and flung his saddle to the animal's back. He rode away, directionless, disturbed. Riding, sometimes a man could work the kinks out of his mind. Riding, his problems sometimes assume a simplicity impossible under other circumstances. But today, Tom found no answers.

III

In two hours of riding, Tom reached the Cady shack. Smaller by far than it had seemed when he went away, it nestled now almost hidden by the encroaching brush. Its door had fallen off, and wild pigs had made their home inside. The dirt floor was rooted up and the ragged bedding was scattered and shredded.

Cady stood in the doorway, sad and moody with memory of the old days, and of old Matt, his father. Now Matt was dead and the old days were gone forever. Matt had been hard. You had to be hard to wrest a living out of the brush, hard and fearless and tough, afraid of no man, of no living thing.

Like McGuire, Matt had never quite forgotten his wife, not quit blaming the thicket for killing her. But he had not drowned his sadness in drink as McGuire had. Matt had compensated for it by giving a little more to his son. He'd taught Tom to ride in the brush, or to move through it afoot as silently as an Indian. But Tom had gone away to war. What had been eating Matt that day in Matadero? Loneliness? Sadness because both wife and son were gone?

Worry? It didn't sound like Matt to go hog wild the way he had.

Tom wandered into the shack. On impulse and out of deep-dredged memory, he put a hand into the eaves where the bunk had been, and found a carved wood horse almost covered with dust. Reflectively he blew the dust from it and rubbed it against his sleeve. How long had it been there? Matt had made it for him when he was only a toddler, and he hadn't seen it in years.

A wave of affection washed over him, and a feeling of loss. Matt was dead. The hands that had carved this toy were still. Tom's face twisted. Why had he gone away and fought in the war? To be beaten, humiliated, starved, and impoverished? Were these good reasons? No. Then why had he fought? What had he gained? Nothing remained of Matt or of the only home Tom remembered. Was Tom's heritage to be only a toy he'd played with as a boy and the tarnished memory of a man who had once been so good to him but who had died a murderer?

His face grew hard, but softened gradually with the persistent memory of his father. His deep-set gray eyes grew warm, and his wide mouth farther widened and curved into a smile. Life with Matt had been good, for all its hardness. There had been respect and liking between them—and a great understanding.

Tom went out and mounted his horse. For a minute or so he just sat, staring moodily at the cabin. Why had Matt sold out? Why would Matt need money? Something about it didn't ring true. Matt had been no killer and he hadn't been insane. He'd have held this place for Tom—unless Matt had thought his son was dead.

Tom reined around abruptly and impatiently. He rode back toward McGuire's, depressed and puzzled, but sure of one thing now, at least. He wasn't leaving the thicket and to hell with anyone who tried to make him leave. The thicket was home. Here were his crowding boyhood memories, the only memories he wanted to keep.

In early evening, more relaxed than he had been all day, he came into the clearing at McGuire's, dismounted, and turned his horse into the corral. Doc's horse was there, nuzzling a few forkfuls of hay that had been pitched over the fence. Another horse stood saddled outside the corral, trying to reach through for a wisp of hay. Every now and then, when he succeeded, McGuire's horse would lay back his ears.

There was a small scuffle between Tom's horse and McGuire's, but afterward they stood at opposite ends of the pile of hay, content to eye each other warily while they ate.

Tom went to the house. Doc sat on the bench. He said: "Hazel's got company."

"Do I know him?"

Doc shook his head. "Don't see how you could. Came after you left. Name's Roy Stutz."

Tom sat down on the bench. He fished a near-empty sack of tobacco from his pocket, eyed it thoughtfully as though measuring its dwindling contents, then regretfully packed a stubby pipe and lighted it. He sensed a peculiar tenseness in McGuire.

"Hazel don't like him and neither do I," the old man said.

"Then why don't you run him off?"

McGuire shrugged eloquently, as if the answer were self-evident.

Tom asked: "Who is he?"

"Carpetbagger. He's Major De Chelly's god-damn' snoop. Tied in some way or another with Schofield, but I'm damned if I know how."

Tom knew the kind. There were plenty of them all through the South, pursuing their crooked schemes under the bought protection of the military. But Tom couldn't help being puzzled by McGuire's odd manner. McGuire kept studying Tom covertly, as though trying to decide something in his mind.

An almost sly quality entered Doc's voice as he said: "He's mean, this Stutz. Purely mean. Lordy, how I'd like. . . ."

"What?"

"Nothing."

Tom pulled at his pipe, wondering at the uneasiness that possessed him. The sky faded as the sun sank below the horizon. Inside the house, he could hear the murmur of voices, Hazel's and a deeper one. After a time, the pitch of both voices rose, as though they were quarreling.

Gray dusk crept across the land. At last the house was silent, save for the angry tread of a man's feet across the floor. The door beside Tom yanked open and a man came out, cramming his hat down over his ears.

Doc McGuire said: "This here's a neighbor of ours, Stutz, Tom Cady, home from the war. He ain't covered with glory, mebbe, but at least he fought for somethin' he believed in."

Tom shot a puzzled look at McGuire, then stood up, and extended his hand. Stutz ignored it, eyeing Cady's uniform contemptuously. He said: "The war's over and it's time some of you damned heroes forgot it."

Tom clenched his teeth. He knew the man was angry because of his fight with Hazel, and because of being baited by Doc, but he didn't like having it taken out on him. He dropped his hand, and a little core of irritation began to build in him.

Doc chuckled uneasily. He said: "Tom's goin' to stay here with us a spell. His own place belongs to Schofield now. Tom says mebbe he'll skin a few steers." Tom thought he detected something deliberately challenging in the Doc's tone, as if he wanted to provoke a fight. But in the faint dusk light, he couldn't read the old man's expression.

Stutz was silent, glowering.

Doc persisted. "He was beat up some, over to Schofield's place. But he's young and tough, and Hazel patched him up real good. I reckon he'll be here a spell . . . leastwise until he's all healed up. He knew Hazel before the war."

On the surface it seemed innocent, just conversation to pass the time at the end of day. Yet Tom could not rid himself of the impression that everything McGuire said was for the purpose of baiting Stutz.

Still Stutz said nothing. Then he began breathing hard. At last he burst out hoarsely: "He'll not stay here, by God! You, Cady! Saddle up and ride. Get out of the country. Hazel's mine, you understand?"

There it was. Another challenge, and why? Because Stutz had quarreled with Hazel and because McGuire had teased him. But once laid down, it was beyond recall.

Tom felt a sudden impatience. He said rashly: "This country's sure changed since I left it. All the damned trash north of the Mason-Dixon line. . . ."

He got no chance to finish. Stutz's fist lashed out, catching him on the side of the head. It drove him down into the dirt and skidded him out across the yard.

Stutz didn't move, but he repeated his harsh demand: "Get out of the country, Johnny. Now, while you've got the chance."

Tom sat on the ground until his head cleared. Then he

got up. McGuire came across the yard and peered closely into his face. He turned quickly to Stutz. "Come on, you two. Out behind the barn. Just as well if Hazel don't have to watch this."

He started out across the yard. Stutz followed, with a venomous, gloating glare at Tom as he passed. Tom fell in behind, feeling much as he had a time or two as a boy, heading out into the brush behind the schoolhouse to have it out with someone or other. Yet there was a difference. The craziness in him now was something he'd never experienced as a boy. It mounted with each passing second. It was his full outrage at injustice and persecution.

They reached the barn and went behind it. Stutz turned, saying heavily: "Last chance, Johnny. I ain't Schofield. With me it's for keeps."

"Man," Tom said, "you push too hard and I've had all the pushing I'll stand."

Stutz laughed. "You'll leave, Johnny. You'll leave if you have to crawl."

Anger flared like a bonfire in Cady's mind. He said: "You're a liar. Besides, there's something else."

"What else?"

"I owe you something. A clout on the side of the head."

He was breathing fast and shallow now. The angry blood raced through his veins. But he spoke once more. He said: "Come on, carpetbagger. Come on. Collect what I owe you with a little interest."

IV

Stutz removed his hat and shrugged out of his coat. He flung them to the ground without taking his eyes from

Tom, who stood waiting warily. Tom knew, now, how foolish he had been. He was still weak from the beating administered to him by Schofield and his crew. Three ribs were broken and might, under the right kind of blow, splinter and puncture lungs or other vital organs. Stutz was big enough to give Tom trouble even had Tom been strong and unhurt. Shoulder muscles rippled under his thin shirt. His neck was a column of muscle and his legs, though tapered and trim, bespoke great strength and agility. Tom recognized him as a man who had fought half a hundred brawls, a man to whom fighting was second nature. He began to grin at Tom the way a cat grins at a saucer of cream.

Tom glanced at McGuire, more than a little puzzled at the way Doc had maneuvered him into this. *I hope you're satisfied,* he thought, and returned his attention to the carefully advancing Stutz.

Moonlight put a yellow glow in the eastern sky as the moon poked its rim above the thicket. In the little clearing behind the sagging barn they circled, wary as two wild beasts, each looking for an opening, an opportunity. The air was silent save for the soft sounds of their rapid breathing. Tom's heart thumped almost audibly in his chest.

He studied his man, trying to decide on the best tactics for fighting him. Stutz's hair, cropped so short it might have been shaven no more than a month ago, was as black and stiff as wire. His black eyes held a mocking travesty of humor that Tom supposed was habitual. Stutz was clean-shaven, although his beard made a heavy blue shadow on his chin and jowls.

Stutz chuckled. "You said something about owing, Johnny. Why don't you pay off?"

The words scarcely cleared his mouth before Tom

launched himself. Like a striking snake, his right hand darted out to smash Stutz's lips against his teeth.

Stutz grunted. He spat explosively at Tom's feet. He rushed, but Tom avoided him nimbly. His quick movements brought stabbing pains to Tom's injured side, but he knew now that his only chance of survival lay in adopting the slashing tactics of the wolf. Slash and retreat. Slash and retreat. Never come to grips.

Stutz lowered his head like a bull and rushed, and this time Tom met him with a solid left and right before he darted aside.

Stutz's cursing stopped. Saving his breath, he was now silent except for the harsh intake and exhalation of his lungs. Every now and again he spat, to clear his mouth of blood.

Tom, so far, had not been hit. Yet the fight was taking its terrible toll of him in spite of that. His side was a sheet of fire, and his belly tied into sympathetic knots. His lungs ached for want of air. Tom's head felt light. He had almost the same feeling of desperation he'd had at Schofield's the other day. He knew he lacked the strength to put Stutz down. Not tonight. He knew only a miracle could save his life.

Perhaps McGuire thought so, too, for he turned and went quickly back to the house. When he came back, he held a rifle in his hands.

Tom lashed Stutz half a dozen more times with his fists, not telling blows, but infuriating ones, for each left his mark on Stutz's face. *If I can get him mad enough,* Tom thought, *he'll go crazy.*

Stutz began to growl deeply in his throat. He spat obscenity and curses at Tom. "You fight like all the yellow-bellied Rebs . . . runnin'. Stand, damn you, stand!"

Tom didn't answer, but the rawest kind of anger rankled in him now. He'd asked for this fight no more than he'd asked for the savage beating at Schofield's the other day. He was a soldier come home, a man who wanted only peace and work and sleep and enough to eat. Three years had he lived with violence. Three years had he lived with death. Now it seemed he must live with them some more. Caution gave way to outrage. He darted in, slashed Stutz's face, and darted out again. When the man rushed him, Tom gave ground, but always his fists were punishing, cutting, slashing.

He could feel the growing wrath in Stutz—like an aura of something tangible that surrounded the man—almost a smell. Stutz's face was bruised and swelling, and, as yet, Tom had no mark on him more serious than a bruise.

The moon's full circle lay now upon the horizon, yellow as the yolk of an egg, big as a copper washtub. Doc leaned against the barn, rifle cradled in his arms, watching Tom as though he were fascinated. His mouth hung open and he was breathing fast.

The time came, as Tom had known it would, when Stutz lost all control of his reason. Fury replaced thought in his mind. He lowered his head and, with arms outstretched, rushed at Tom.

Tom leaped aside, feeling the clawing of one of Stutz's hands on his coat. Whirling then, pivoting, he brought his two clasped hands down like a club against the back of Stutz's neck. Stutz fell like a steer. He rolled, and lay still.

McGuire chortled exultantly: "You done it, boy! I knew you could! You done it!"

"Not yet."

Stutz was stirring, rolling, groaning a little. He came to his knees, shaking his head as if to clear it. McGuire yelled:

"Get him, Tom! Get the damned Yankee leech!"

Tom didn't move, other than to glance again at Doc. Stutz stayed on his knees, shaking his head. His two hands went to the back of his neck, apparently to rub the numbness from it. Doc screeched suddenly: "His knife! He keeps his knife back there! Get out of the way, Tom!"

Now Tom knew why Doc had gone for the rifle. Tom rushed toward Stutz, who was still on his knees. The hands came away from Stutz's neck, and the right one held a gleaming, eight-inch blade. Tom saw the triumphant grimace of Stutz's mouth. He saw the gleaming teeth, and the lips drawn back, and he stopped abruptly.

Stutz came to his feet and began his slow advance. He held the knife at waist level, a little away from his body, with the cutting edge up. His left arm, bent at the elbow, stood out from his body, the hand like a claw. He said: "What do you think they'll do to me, Cady, for opening you up and letting your guts run out? Hang me? Hell, no, they won't. De Chelly will probably give me a medal. So run, Johnny. Run while you've still got a chance. Ain't that the way you fought the war, Johnny? Runnin'?"

Tom stood his ground between McGuire and Stutz.

Doc shouted: "Get outta the way, Tom! He'll drop that knife or I'll blow his guts out!" But Tom did not move.

When Stutz was half a dozen feet away, Tom jumped backward. With a flat-hand blow he sent Doc sprawling. Then he whirled to face Stutz. His stomach felt empty and knotted. Was this what he had ridden all the way from Georgia for? Had he gone through three years of war, only to die here in ugly anonymity on the dirty ground behind McGuire's barn? He began to weave, ready to leap to left or right. His action seemed to infuriate Stutz further, for he abandoned his cautious approach and broke into a shambling run.

Tom stopped weaving. His muscles knotted, as though they could halt the bite of the steel in Stutz's hand. He saw the triumph that gleamed in the agate eyes. He saw the knife and its flashing blade, and heard McGuire's scrambling and gasp of dismay.

What happened then was almost too fast for the eye to follow. Tom stopped, and appeared to dive forward, directly at the point of the knife. Doc's breathing stopped altogether. Then Stutz's powerful form seemed to lift from the earth. A yell that had no words escaped his lips. He flew over Tom's head. He crashed to the earth some ten feet behind Tom, and there he lay still.

Doc rushed forward, ready to catch Tom as he fell. The rifle clattered to the ground. But Tom did not fall. He swayed, his breath a rapid bellows of exhaustion, but he did not fall.

Doc whirled him around. With trembling hands he probed the gashed back of Tom's coat. He withdrew his hand and stared at it with amazement. "You didn't even get scratched!"

"Uhn-huh. I got under him and heaved. I've done that to men with bayonets on their guns, but never before to a man with a knife."

McGuire picked up the rifle and advanced cautiously toward the still form of Stutz. Tom heard the hammer draw back and cock. Then McGuire stopped. He toed Stutz over his back and breathed: "Tom, come here."

Tom walked over and looked down. The knife was buried to the hilt in Stutz's chest.

All strength seemed to go out of Tom's body. He staggered to the barn wall and leaned against it. No. He hadn't returned from the war to die squalidly behind McGuire's barn. He had returned for the hangman's noose.

Sheriff Durand might conceivably listen to a plea of self-defense, but the major of the bluebelly troops would not. This was a time when the conquerors dared not countenance violence against themselves, when no man who had fought for the Confederate cause expected justice from the occupying troops. McGuire's testimony that it was an accident would be worthless, and Hazel, who might have been believed, was somewhere deep in the huge house. She had heard not a word of this nor seen what happened.

Tom lowered his head into his hands. For a moment, panic touched him, and then resentment began to grow. What was all this about, anyway? Why Schofield's senseless animosity? Why Durand's mild insistence that he leave the country? Why McGuire's sly promotion of this fight between Tom and Stutz? He turned on Doc savagely. "Damn you, what was all that about? You engineered that fight!"

Doc didn't answer. Tom seized him by the coat front and shook him.

"Why, damn you? Why?"

Doc pulled away. "I didn't aim to see him killed," he whined. "I swear I didn't. I only wanted him whipped good. I figured, if you whipped him, maybe the son-of-a-bitch would stay away from here."

"Because of Hazel? Can't she handle him? It sounded to me like she was doing all right."

"So far she's done all right," Doc said defensively, "but you didn't know Stutz. If I'd be gone sometime when he came. . . ." He was briefly silent, watching Tom's face while he kept his own carefully shadowed. He added: "Hell, it was getting so he practically lived here. Hazel was tired of it and so was I."

Tom didn't know why, but he had a feeling that Doc was lying. There was something else, some other reason Doc had wanted Stutz whipped. Maybe he did want Stutz to stay away, but it wasn't because of Hazel. Tom felt sure of that. He growled: "So you used me, is that it?"

Doc didn't answer, and it didn't really matter anyway. Tom was finished. He had but two choices now, neither of them good. He could run, or he could haul Stutz's body into Matadero and take his chances with the bluebelly law. He laughed bitterly. Either way he was finished. If he ran, they'd catch him. If he stayed, they'd hang him.

Doc said softly—"What now, Tom?"—and, oddly, Doc's voice sounded calm as though panic had fled and he was again in full control of himself.

"You mean am I going to commit suicide by hauling him into town? I'm not."

"You figurin' to run?"

Tom shrugged. He couldn't answer that even for himself.

Then Doc's voice became wheedling and sly. "Nobody knows about this but you an' me, Tom. Why don't we just drag him out in the bush and bury him?"

Tom stared at him.

"I'll get a shovel," Doc said decisively.

Tom waited, confused and exhausted. Presently the old man appeared, carrying a shovel in place of his rifle. He said: "Drag him over here."

He picked up Stutz's hat and coat and walked off into the brush. Tom picked up the polished, booted feet of Stutz and followed, dragging the body behind him. Instinct told him that this was wrong, but he knew what would happen to him if he dared carry Stutz into Matadero. Months in the stinking jail. Then a farce of a trial. After that, the hangman's noose in the public square. This was the only other way.

Doc halted about 200 yards from the house. He marked out a grave on the ground. Wheezing, he began to dig. "It's got to be deep," he panted, "else the hogs will root him out."

The old man tired quickly. Tom took the shovel from him. He began to dig, and within moments perspiration beaded his face. When he was down two feet, Doc spelled him, and, after Tom caught his breath, he took over again.

An hour later, the grave was six feet deep. Tom cut himself some steps in its side and climbed out. His ribs were now a steady, blazing bed of coals.

McGuire threw in Stutz's coat and hat, then rolled Stutz in after them as though he had never been a man at all. Tom began to throw dirt into the open grave. From time to time he jumped in and trampled it down.

Doc took the shovel from him and finished. He leveled off the spot, and then pitched the remaining dirt into the nearby mesquite. Tom gathered leaves and brush and skillfully covered the grave with them.

They left the place and walked silently back to the house. McGuire let Stutz's horse go free. Already a couple of hogs were snuffing and rooting at the spot where Stutz had bled and died. McGuire chased them away with the shovel.

Reaction from the fight began to set in with Tom. His hands trembled and he felt sick at his stomach. He felt unclean as he never had during the war. This was shameful, secret business, for all that it was not his fault.

Standing beside the door, he could hear Hazel stirring around in the kitchen, washing the supper dishes. He was glad she'd neither seen nor heard the fight.

Doc sat down on the bench as though nothing of particular importance had happened. Yet there seemed to be tension in him, too. He repeated his earlier question: "What now?"

"How do I know?" Anger made Tom's voice strong, although he held its pitch low. "Should I run away because a damn' carpetbagger fell on his own knife? I didn't kill him. And I won't run as though I had."

"All right. But what are you going to do? You've got to eat."

Tom said patiently: "I told you before. Hides are fetching a good price in Indianola. And the way this brush country is overstocked, a man doesn't have to look far for cattle to skin."

McGuire shook his head. "You think Schofield will let you alone? He claims every critter for fifty miles. He'll catch you once and you'll have had it."

"You got a better idea?" Tom asked sourly.

"Mebbe I have." Again there was that slyness in McGuire's voice, slyness that concealed some deeper purpose. "You want to get even with Schofield for that beating, don't you?"

Tom thought of Schofield, but his anger was tinged with disgust. He didn't like Doc's slyness, and he didn't like the way Doc had used him tonight. He was becoming wary. He said: "All right. Let's hear it. But don't use me again, Doc."

Doc said: "What Schofield can do, someone else can do. Start building for yourself, Tom. There's tens of thousands of cattle there in the thicket between Austin and the Gulf, cattle that mostly have never seen a man. They belong to the one who brands 'em."

"For that a man needs money . . . and help . . . and to be let alone by the troops."

McGuire laughed. "You think Schofield had any of those things when he first came here? Hell, no. He didn't even have a headquarters until he bought your old man out. He brags he had fifty dollars and a horse when he rode in here. Know what he's got now? A crew of six men, your old man's four thousand acre ranch, and his brand on five thousand cattle. You can do the same."

Tom frowned at Doc. "Are you suggesting a partnership? Is that it, Doc?"

"Why not? Listen, Tom, a man might start out with a penny-ante operation. That's the way Butterfield started. But there's millions in it. Millions! There's an empire here for the man with the guts to build it."

Tom studied the old man carefully. The moon shone fully upon Doc's face, which was lighted by more than moonlight. Again Tom had the odd feeling that Doc wanted something besides the thing he said he wanted. Tom said: "What do you want with money or an empire, either, Doc? You don't give a damn about money. You never have."

"It's not for me. It's for Hazel, so that, when I die, she can go away. She's scared, Tom, and a scared woman gets hard as nails. I wouldn't want to see Hazel like that."

Tom shrugged. He couldn't shake the suspicion that he was being used again, yet neither could he doubt feeling that here was a chance to strike back at Schofield where it would hurt the most. And striking back, infuriating the man, perhaps he would learn something about the way his father had died. There had to be more to Matt's death than a berserker rampage in the plaza at Matadero. Somehow or other Tom couldn't visualize Matt's going berserk. There had to be some reason behind it.

He looked at Doc again, curiously. There was a puzzle here that interested him, too. He nodded sourly. "All right.

What have I got to lose?"

Doc grinned up at him, a kind of triumph in his eyes. Tom couldn't help wondering what Doc would have done if he'd said no. Would Doc have threatened him with exposure over the killing of Stutz? Or would Doc have let him go? Tom didn't know.

"Good," Doc said abruptly. "Now go on up and get some sleep. We'll talk it out in the morning."

Tom went in, barely glancing at Hazel before he tramped up the stairs to his room.

V

When her father came in, Hazel studied him closely. "What happened between you two and Roy? Did you quarrel?"

McGuire shook his head. He shuffled over to the stove, got a cup from the shelf above it, and poured it full of coffee. He cut himself a slice of bread and plastered it thickly with jam. Then he sat down at the table.

"What was the matter with Tom?"

"Tired, mebbe." McGuire spoke with his mouth half full. He sipped the scalding coffee, not real coffee but a substitute made by roasting beans. After a while he said: "Tom's goin' to stay."

She didn't know whether to be angry or glad. As always of late, she found herself wondering at her father's motives. "Stay for what? There's no work here for Tom."

"Mebbe we'll brand a few cattle. Everybody else is doing it."

"Everybody, or just Schofield?"

"Well, Schofield, I guess. But we got the same rights he's got. All the brush cattle don't belong to him."

Concern touched her for the first time. She sat down at the table across from him, a tall and pretty girl whose face was still and cold from gnawing fear. She noticed that he didn't meet her eyes steadily. He seemed to be trying to slide away. She said: "What are you up to, Pa?"

He retreated into the secretiveness of a small boy. He wiped his mouth with the back of a nervous hand. His voice rose in a whine. "I ain't up to nothin', damn it. You been after me for years to do something that amounts to something. All right. I'm doing it. That's all there is to it."

"But you're a doctor, not a brush popper."

He laughed bitterly. "I *was* a doctor." A flush tinted his whiskery old face. "Now I'm a peddler, selling whiskey to all comers, paying half of it in taxes to that stinking De Chelly. Taxes, hell! It's graft, that's what it is."

Hazel tried to puzzle him out. She thought his eyes seemed clearer than they had a year ago, as though he had stopped drinking, or almost had. Yet she knew this was impossible, for he still came reeling in most nights to collapse and sleep on the horsehair sofa in the small room that had been her mother's sewing room just off the kitchen. She felt a surge of compassion for him, followed immediately by a twinge of exasperation and suspicion. You don't live with a man eighteen years without getting to know him, and Hazel knew her father as a devious fraud. When he was of a mind to, he could pull the wool over anyone's eyes but hers, and yet she knew his grief for her mother was real, perhaps the only real thing in his life. It had driven him to drink, to neglect his profession and his pride. He had gone steadily downhill after her death and had kept going until. . . . Hazel frowned a little, trying to place the time when the elusive change had begun in her father. She guessed it had been about a year ago—maybe a little more than that. About the time De Chelly came to Matadero with his troops. About the time law was scrapped for vengefulness and graft. About the time Schofield began to grow from a penny-ante, greedy little brush popper into a big man with money to spend and a way of getting the things he wanted through De Chelly and Stutz.

Hazel shook her head wearily, getting up. "All right, Pa. But it's a mistake."

She walked around the kitchen for a few minutes, troubled and vaguely worried. Then, hands on hips, she turned to her father again.

"Why, Pa? Why right now?"

"Been worryin' about you, mebbe. What'd you do if somethin' was to happen to me? Where'd you go? We got no money, De Chelly sees to that, and nobody in their right mind would buy this place. You'd end up marryin' somebody like Roy Stutz . . . or not marryin' at all. Mebbe you'd end up in some *cantina* in Matadero."

"But why now?" A wave of concern washed over her. "Are you sick, Pa?"

"Uhn-uh. I'm fine. It just seemed that mebbe Tom Cady . . . well, it seemed like he might be the one who could take on Schofield and get the job done."

"He's agreed to do it?"

McGuire grinned. "He's agreed, all right. Tomorrow we'll dig out them few gold pieces we been savin'. We'll go to Matadero an' buy us a thing or two. Then we'll start."

Hazel watched him rise, yawning, from the table. He disappeared into the depths of the house, as Tom had done.

She went outside and sat on the bench in the moonlight. Leaning back against the wall of the house, she stared up at the sky full of stars. There was softness in her face, now that no one could see, and the dreaming of a girl.

She thought of Stutz, and suddenly her body felt cold. She thought of a life that went on like this until its end, and she could not repress a shudder. Then she thought of Tom, and the faintest of smiles touched the corners of her mouth. She began to hope, for the first time. Perhaps her father would do the impossible. With Cady's help, he really might build something here in the brush. She envisioned cattle herds that stretched as far as the eye could see. She envisioned herself riding in a carriage, dressed in silks like the ladies in Matadero, and carrying a small, ridiculous parasol.

The night was warm, for December. Its softness caressed her cheeks and its light breeze stirred her night-black hair. Her lips, so full and red, began to smile freely.

At last she rose and returned to the kitchen. She picked up the lamp and started for her room and in its harsh yellow light her face was hard again, and cold. Not yet was the time for hope. Not yet. Wait until time had proved Doc's words to be true, his newfound ambition to be steadfast. Wait until. . . . Suddenly, then, fear laid clammy hands on Hazel. Her father's plan was a fool's plan for committing suicide. Schofield would never allow his supremacy in the brush to be challenged. Schofield would kill if need be, and would go unpunished if he did. Cady might be a good man and a strong one, but who could fight a ruthlessness such as Schofield's? What one man could fight seven, and the law as well? No. The idea was foolish and both Doc and Tom must know it. If they persisted in it, they'd both be dead inside of a month.

Exhaustion kept Tom asleep until almost nine o'clock in the morning. When he finally did awake, the house was still. He dressed painfully, favoring his hurt ribs, and went down

49

the stairs to the kitchen. Hazel was gone and so was her father.

Since first awakening, Stutz's death and the macabre disposal of his body had been foremost in Tom's thoughts. He considered saddling his horse and riding out. But not for long. A kind of defiance was building up in him, a reckless disregard for consequences. He'd done nothing that could be considered even remotely wrong since his arrival. To hell with Schofield and De Chelly. To hell with Durand. Why did they all want to be rid of him, assuming that Stutz had spoken last night for De Chelly? What threat did he constitute?

He poured himself a cup of black, rancid-tasting coffee that was simmering on the stove. He cut himself a thick slice of bread and plastered it liberally with jam. He sat down at the table, wolfed the bread, then sipped the coffee moodily.

Last night's violence plagued him, put a bad taste in his mouth that not even the coffee could wash away. Stutz was dead, buried out in the brush. How long before De Chelly and his troops came snooping around? How long before shrewd old Sheriff Durand came to ask his carefully phrased questions? Tom finished his coffee and went out into the sunlight. He sat down on the bench, and packed his stubby pipe with the remains of his tobacco, and went on thinking.

There was a pattern here somewhere. The pieces would fit together if a man could find them all. Perhaps the way to bring the pieces together was to treat Schofield, Durand, and De Chelly the way Doc had treated Stutz last night. Bait Schofield by branding cattle he considered his own. Bait Durand by staying in the face of Durand's thinly veiled order to leave. Bait De Chelly with Stutz, who had disappeared from the face of the earth. He smoked, and occasionally scratched at the four-day growth of reddish whiskers upon his jaw.

He heard no sound but the soft rooting of a couple of nearby hogs, the usual stirrings of wild things in the brush. But suddenly he felt the hairs on the back of his neck stir. He knew he was not alone.

Carefully concealing his nervousness, he looked around at the brush of the thicket. He looked down the road that led away, and at a narrow path that wound into the brush toward the spot where Stutz was buried. In one respect, staring into the brush is like staring into nearly complete darkness. If you strain your eyes and try too hard, you see nothing. The trick is to relax, and, when you find something that interests you, to look at it slantwise.

Tom's eyes picked out a spot slightly darker than the rest, and at last he saw the dim, plain outline of a man. His muscles tensed, but he did not stir. He had no gun, and, against a man who had, he was helpless.

The figure moved, accompanied by a crackling of brush, and a voice called out from the thicket: *"Buenos días, amigo."*

Tom shouted harshly: "Come out of there!"

"Sí." The brush parted and a man came out.

Tom said coldly: "How long you been there?"

"Un momento." The speaker was slight and swarthy, pockmarked and hollow-cheeked. His teeth flashed as he smiled, firm and white. A sparse black beard covered his chin. His eyes were dark, secret things even as they sparkled their amusement. He wore tight buckskin pants, black with smoke and campfire grease, an unusually dirty shirt that appeared to have once been white, and heavy duck brush jacket. His face and neck were shiny with sweat and skin oils.

Tom Cady inspected his eyes first, judging the man's intentions by what he saw there, and he relaxed perceptibly afterward. After that, more leisurely, Tom appraised the pouch-laden belt and the gun that hung at the Mexican's waist. If the man's trousers were high-waisted, the gun belt was not. It hung around the slim hips a full five inches below the trouser waistband. On the right side it sagged even farther. A rawhide thong tied the bottom of the holster to the man's thigh. Tom had never seen a gun worn quite that way before. As a matter of fact, you saw few belt guns here in the brush. A man might have a rifle, but few owned revolvers or even old-style pistols. Officers carried them in the war, but Tom had not been an officer.

"What do you want?" he asked with neutral wariness.

The Mexican's teeth flashed. He shrugged expressively. "What does any man want from another? *Sociedad, amigo.* Companionship. Talk. It is lonely in the brush for my kind of man." His sharp dark eyes kept watching the two hogs out beside the barn, rooting at the spot where Stutz had bled and died.

"And what kind of man are you?"

The Mexican's grin seemed to tighten, but he said easily enough: "A man who wonders why hogs root so deeply beside a barn. A man who can tell from the sound when a razorback smells blood."

Tom stirred on the bench and said softly: "Maybe a man who sees and hears too much."

"Perhaps." The Mexican changed the subject abruptly. "This is a magnificent house to be sitting here in the thicket. You live in it alone?"

"No." Tom felt the unexpected run of his relief. "It's the house of Doc McGuire."

The Mexican's eyebrows lifted quizzically. "The one

with the so beautiful daughter?"

"You know her?"

"Let us say I know of her. But who does not? *Por Dios,*
beauty is a rare thing in the brush country and news of a
blossoming flower travels far."

Tom frowned. "You're too damned smooth with words.
Maybe you better get on your feet and move along."

The Mexican showed no resentment. He shrugged
again, and it became apparent to Tom that the shrug was
just a habit, a mannerism that expressed nothing at all.
"*Bueno, amigo.* If I am not welcome here, then I will go.
Perhaps I will find the companionship I seek with *el sheriff*
in Matadero. Perhaps we will discuss rooting hogs and a
lonely house where the guests are sent away."

Tom grinned. "Not you! You wouldn't go within a mile
of the sheriff. Good bye, my friend."

The Mexican looked hurt, then suddenly returned
Tom's grin. He murmured: "You are no fool, for all your
lack of years. You know that Miguel Ortiz has no love for
the law."

"I was sure of it."

Miguel moved into the shade and squatted comfortably
against the wall of the house. He fished in his shirt pocket
and found two long, thin, twisted black cigars. He handed
one to Tom, lighted his own, and puffed luxuriously.

"Let us rest in the shade, *compañero.* When it is dark,
then I will go."

VI

Near sundown, Hazel and Doc McGuire returned. Doc
rode his ancient bay mare, but Hazel rode a trim *bayo*

coyote, a dun gelding with a black mane and tail. Fifty yards behind the pair rode two men who Tom had never seen before.

Tom helped Hazel to the ground, but she did not warm at his gallantry. She seemed too preoccupied for that. However, she did not miss Miguel, standing so unobtrusively beside the door. Indeed, both she and Doc had been watching the Mexican warily ever since they rode out of the mesquite.

McGuire untied a sack that had been lashed behind his saddle. He laid it on the ground beside the door. Then he led the two animals off toward the narrow creek for water. The pair of strangers followed him, although one kept glancing back over his shoulder at Tom.

Miguel came forward and swept off his hat. "Present me, *señor.*"

Tom said: "He claims his name is Miguel Ortiz."

Much frank admiration showed in the Mexican's eyes as he gazed at Hazel. So much so that she flushed.

"What do you want?" she said.

Miguel sighed. "Such an unfriendly land. I want nothing, *señorita.* It is only that a man living alone in the thicket hungers for the sight of other men, and sometimes grows hungry for the sight of a woman as beautiful as yourself." He smiled disarmingly.

Hazel's expression did not soften. Obviously she did not like the way things were going. She started toward the kitchen door. "Supper will be ready soon," she said, and paused just long enough to ask Tom: "How do you feel?"

"All right."

She nodded, and went on. Then Doc shuffled up, followed by the two strangers. Cady inspected them carefully.

The one who had seemed to take such an interest in him

before was tall for a Mexican, and very slender. His narrow shoulders stooped forward and his eyes were at once furtive and bold. His face was thin, his forehead high. When he removed his hat to mop his brow, Tom saw that he was partly bald, but that there was no gray in his hair. His style of dress matched Miguel's except that he wore a pair of cotton trousers and straw sandals on his bare feet. Tom felt vaguely uneasy under the man's steady scrutiny.

Doc said: "This one's Tonio Polidoro."

Tom nodded, and Doc said: "The other is Ivy Peebles."

Peebles was a small, oldish man, mild of expression, probably equally mild of disposition. His eyes were a pale, washed-out blue, with the vagueness usually associated with one who drinks excessively. Tom thought he was more the sort you'd expect to see measuring cloth in a mercantile store or swamping a saloon than riding the thicket for cattle. Yet, studying Peebles, he thought he detected a deep-hidden core of toughness in the man. He liked Peebles at once.

Doc rummaged in the sack that had been tied behind his saddle. Out of the sack he brought a walnut-handled pistol. He handed it to Tom.

Tom examined it curiously. It was a .36-caliber Colt Patent revolver. Doc brought out a holster and belt, after that bullet pouch, powder flask, and another small pouch containing percussion caps. He also brought out a small keg containing powder, a bar of lead, and a bullet mold.

Tom balanced the gun in his hand. He looked at Doc, at Miguel, at Peebles and Polidoro. He had an odd suspicion that, if he accepted the gun, he would be committing himself to something that might eventually destroy him, and yet what choice did he have? He'd come home, wanting only a job and a chance to work in peace. Schofield and Stutz had changed all that. They had made it plain that there could be no peace for him.

Doc was watching him slyly, as if he also knew that Tom Cady stood at a crossroads. The gun had a lovely, deadly feel to it, gleaming so dully black and silver in the sunset's glow. Tom noticed that Miguel Ortiz's eyes were bright with interest.

"It is like mine, *señor,* but newer," Miguel Ortiz said. "A better gun than that has not been made. Feel its balance."

Perhaps Doc sensed a wavering in Tom, for he said: "It's only a tool, Tom, same way a surgeon's knife is a tool. It's useful, too, like your horse and rope. And that's all. A gun doesn't make a man a killer. It's something in the heart that does that."

Tom hefted the gun. *What a temptation for the heart,* he thought.

Doc said softly: "You were in the war. Did they send you into battle with nothing but your bare hands? Look at it this way. Do you judge a war by its size and the number of men involved? Isn't a little war as deadly for the men who die in it as a big one? There's a war in the thicket, Tom. You've seen enough to know that."

Still Tom hesitated. Once he strapped on this gun, he would use it. Someday he would have to use it. The likes of Schofield and Stutz would force him to. His jaw hardened. But then it occurred to him that a gun in his hand last night would have saved a life—Stutz's life.

Miguel stepped close. He extended a hand. "May I see it, *señor?*"

Tom handed him the gun. Ortiz took the powder flask from his own belt and poured powder into each cylinder chamber. From his own bullet pouch he took bullets, and after that caps. When the gun was loaded, he spun the cylinder and thumbed back the hammer. So swiftly then as to deceive the eye, he brought up the gun and fired. One of the hogs, rooting at the edge of the thicket, squealed loudly and dived for the safety of the brush. The hog shook its head as it ran; it had a small round hole in its ear.

Miguel laughed delightedly and handed the gun back to Tom. "A fine gun. A fine gift. What is it that bothers you, *amigo?*"

For an instant their eyes locked. It was the Mexican who finally looked away. Tom was twenty-two, but his eyes revealed something acquired on a dozen hopeless battlefronts, something no one can name, but which can chill the boldest man who has never endured the horrors of war. Perhaps it was an unconscious emanation of power, of danger. Whatever it was, Doc had seen it in Tom yesterday, and again last night during his fight with Stutz. It was the thing that had made Doc sure that Tom must be the man to wrest an empire from the brush and defeat Schofield doing it.

Miguel murmured: "You try it, *compañero.*"

Tom raised the gun, sighted, and fired. The bullet kicked up dust a dozen yards beyond the rock at which he had aimed. He threw the gun down on the empty sack. "I'll use my hands or a rifle," he said disgustedly, and strode off into the brush.

For a time an uneasy silence lay among the four in the yard. Peebles and Polidoro drifted toward the corral. At last Miguel said: "There is something here I cannot understand. What is it you wish to do with the gun? A murder?"

"Hell, no," Doc said, but the old, sly expression began to creep back into his face. Finally he asked: "You can ride the brush?"

Miguel laughed. "The mesquite, the cat-claw, the agrito, and chapote, they are friends to Miguel Ortiz. They remind a man to be careful. How do you think I came by these scars?" he pointed to his cheek, to an ear half torn away.

"You want a job?"

Miguel shrugged lightly and made a grimace of distaste. "Riding? At twenty a month? No, *señor*. I do not think so."

McGuire looked out across the yard. A scorpion was rattling along at the edge of the thicket, stirring the dry leaves at the foot of a huisache tree. Leaves and scorpion were almost the same color. Doc said: "You see that scorpion over there?"

"But, of course, *señor*."

The scorpion was a full fifteen yards away. Doc murmured: "Can you kill it?"

There was a sudden blur of movement, a sharp report. The scorpion disappeared in a puff of dust. Miguel slid his gun back into its holster.

McGuire licked his lips like a pleased cat. "Could you teach young Cady to use a gun like that?"

"Perhaps. In time. If he would consent."

Doc said: "I'll pay you thirty a month, your keep, and a tenth share in the herd we will gather out of the brush."

Miguel's laugh rang out high and clear, a mocking laugh matched by the mocking light in his eyes. "Suppose I agree, *señor?* And suppose that later I decide to take it all, the herd, the *señorita,* perhaps your life, old man? What then? What would stop me . . . conscience? I have none, *señor*."

Tom Cady spoke from the edge of the thicket. "I'd stop you."

The words were soft, emotionless, almost conversational. Miguel's expression did not change. He even laughed again, but it sounded different somehow. "*Por Dios,*" he said. "I will take this job."

"Why? Why the change of heart?" Doc was scowling now, uncertain.

"Why? Perhaps because I would see the wolf cub become a wolf. I would see his fangs grow sharp. Perhaps, also, I am curious and would find answers to the questions going around in my head. Perhaps I want the cattle you will brand, or the *señorita* whose face is like the wind that comes out of the north. But what matter, *señor*? I will stay and I will teach the young one to use the gift you have brought him. Is that not enough?"

McGuire nodded, suspicion lingering in his manner. He said: "All right. Tomorrow we will start. Tomorrow we begin to build our herd and be damned to anyone that tries to stop us." He turned toward Tom, who still stood at the edge of the brush. "What'll the brand be, Tom?"

Tom shrugged, so the Mexican said: "Ah, make it mean something, *señor*. If I am to have a share, let me suggest the brand. A star, because that is the thing for which you reach. And the cross, perhaps, so that the good God may forgive the way you reach the star."

Over against the blackness of the brush at dusk, Tom Cady snorted his sour disgust. Within him a premonition was growing, a strange unease that he had felt many times during the war. He knew what lay ahead—killing, and hate, and destruction. He consoled himself with the thought that he had no choice, and that what they did was not in itself wrong. Only Schofield could make it wrong.

VII

As the moon began to rise out of the thicket to the east, Hazel came to the door and called them to supper. Tom went to the pump and doused his head, afterwards rubbing his face and neck vigorously. He worked the pump handle for Peebles, Polidoro, Doc, and Miguel, and the five started for the kitchen. From the windows came a feeble glow of lamplight, and from the door a tantalizing odor of frying pork. Then Tom's war-trained ears caught the *clatter* of a cavalry patrol. They were coming hard, apparently in a hurry. Panic reached him. He halted in his tracks. His first impulse was to run for cover. Then he remembered that the war was over, and stood his ground.

They pounded into the clearing and reined in, stirring up a cloud of dust that drifted chokingly over the five men on the ground. Durand was with them, and their leader was a tall, middle-aged cavalry major, thin except for a paunchy middle and heavy folds of jowl. The patrol split and spread around the men on the ground.

Durand said: "Let me talk to them, De Chelly. We'll get further."

Tom waited passively.

Durand asked: "What happened to you?"

"Schofield."

"Why?"

"Your guess is as good as mine," Tom said, and was glad Durand couldn't see his face clearly. He braced himself for the moment when Stutz's name would be mentioned, but Durand turned to Doc McGuire.

"We're looking for Roy Stutz," he said. "You seen him, Doc?"

"He was here last night. Left about seven."

Durand looked at Tom again. "Were you here? Did you see him?"

Tom hesitated, trying to think. He should have answered immediately, for De Chelly had been watching him, taking in every detail of his gray Confederate uniform.

De Chelly reined aside. He stopped his horse close beside Tom and said: "Making up lies, Rebel? How'd you like to spend six months in solitary?"

Tom said nothing. He couldn't, and wouldn't, answer questions like that.

"I don't mean Durand's nice clean jail," De Chelly said. "I mean my jail. There's a difference . . . quite a difference."

Here it comes, Tom thought, and waited.

De Chelly's mouth twitched oddly. He said: "I know a number of ways to make a man talk." His voice became smooth and very deadly. "Answer the question, you dirty Rebel son-of-a-bitch."

Tom remained silent. A dull flush began to rise in De Chelly's face. Suddenly he spurred his horse. The horse plunged wildly, bowling Tom over. His forefoot came down on Tom's thigh. Tom yelled with pain.

The horse danced off, but De Chelly controlled him with a cruel hand.

Tom jumped up, disregarding pain. He lunged at De Chelly and seized the man's booted leg. He started to yank, then heard the sound of a revolver cocking not a foot from his head. Doc and Miguel grabbed him by the arms.

Durand's great voice roared: "Wait a minute! God damn it, wait a minute!"

Doc and Miguel dragged Tom back. De Chelly's face was livid. He raised his gun deliberately, aiming at Tom's knees. Durand spurred and reined his plunging horse between De Chelly and Tom. De Chelly began to curse in a droning monotone, his choice of words vilely obscene.

Tom Cady struggled to free himself, but Miguel kept saying softly: "Easy, *compañero.* Do you want to die tonight?

61

Do you want both your knees shattered? Easy, *amigo.*"

Durand held his horse steady between Tom and the major. "Tom," he said urgently, "for God's sake answer the man. Were you here last night? Did you see Stutz?"

"I saw him. He left about seven, like Doc said."

"He's lying," De Chelly said.

Durand turned. "How do you know he's lying? Hell, Major, you can't treat people like this. Now, cool off."

The troopers sat their horses stolidly, doing nothing but surrounding the men on the ground. If it had not been for Durand, all five of them would be dead by now. Durand said soothingly: "Take your patrol on out, Major. Let me talk to them."

For a minute there was only silence in the yard, a tight, uneasy silence, dangerous and deadly. At last the major whirled his horse and galloped from the clearing. The troopers strung out behind, leaving Durand.

Durand frowned at Tom, who had angrily shaken off the restraining hands of Doc and Miguel. "I thought I told you you'd be smart to leave."

"You did."

"So you're not smart. Is that it?"

"Maybe I'm dumb enough to wonder why everybody's in such a sweat. You'd think you and De Chelly and Schofield were afraid of me. Stutz. . . ." Tom halted. He could feel sweat spring out on his face.

Durand said: "Go on, Tom. What were you going to say?"

"Nothing."

"You have a fight with Stutz?"

"What if I did?"

Durand's voice was mild. "Why nothin', son. Unless you killed him."

"I didn't."

"All right." Durand looked at Doc. "Sorry we bothered you." He nudged his horse and rode after the others.

Miguel whistled. "*¡Por Dios!* What was all that about?" he asked innocently, and Doc McGuire exploded.

"Nothin', damn it! Nothin'! Now come on in to supper before it gets cold."

They all followed Doc inside. Miguel was grinning at some secret joke.

They were up two hours before dawn. They ate breakfast before beginning this, their first day of work. Doc stayed behind, having no enthusiasm for riding the thorny thicket, and Tom was content to see him do so. The old man would be more hindrance than help.

In complete darkness, the crew rode out toward a clearing that Tom knew, a clearing not too far from one of the corrals built by his father a decade ago, where the wild cattle of the brush would be grazing at dawn. In silence they rode, and slowly, for a man does not hurry through the thorny tangle in darkness. Half an hour before dawn, they arrived at the chosen spot, which was a kind of brush finger extending out into a grassy clearing of perhaps 100 acres in size.

There they sat their horses and waited patiently for the light. In the first gray light of dawn they could see a bunch of fifty or so gaunt longhorn cattle, grazing out toward the center of the clearing.

Tom whispered: "When we ride out, they'll break for the closest point of brush, which is right here. So they'll be coming directly at us. Pick yourselves a good animal each and drop a rope on him."

Simple instructions for a simple-sounding task—until you realized that here was no domesticated animal, but a completely wild one, fearing and hating man with brute intensity. Here was an animal with horns measuring as much as six feet from tip to tip, weighing as much as 1,200 or 1,300 pounds, all of it hard muscle and sinew and bone. The wild cattle of the brush were sly as wolves, as fearless as cougars, and as fleet-footed in their ponderous way as deer. It took a particular kind of man to ride the brush. It took a peculiar fearlessness, a disregard for personal injury. Each instant you rode this brush country, you rode with death.

Miguel murmured almost soundlessly, an odd pleasure in his voice: "*Sí, amigo.* I see a fine old mossyhorn that I have marked for my own. The *puro negro,* with the horns curving up to the sky. Is not that one fine? Ten years old, if he is a day."

Tom grinned. He had grown to like this Miguel in the time he had known him, for all of Miguel's mocking secretiveness. He said: "Get him then. It is light enough now."

With a sharp cry, Miguel spurred out into the clearing, an open loop of his lariat dangling from his hand. Tom followed, and behind came Polidoro and Ivy Peebles. The great beasts in the clearing raised their shaggy heads and shook their ponderous, wickedly curving horns. Their eyes glared, fierce as those of a javelina, and clouds of steam blew from their snorting nostrils. They flung defiance as they broke into ponderous, but swift motion, thundering like a charge of cavalry directly at the galloping men.

But they were fleeing, for all of that. They simply charged for the nearest thicket cover, which happened to be behind the men who had appeared so suddenly out of nowhere. The cattle split the moment collision seemed inevitable, split around the horsemen because of instinctive, inherited fear of the small, two-legged creatures. Tom's loop went out, hissing like a snake, and dropped over the horns of a red-and-white bull. Another galloped past, so close that the wicked tip of his horn bruised Tom's leg and tore his pants. As his horse set his hoofs, Tom braced himself. He heard Miguel's high yell, and another sound like a pistol shot followed immediately by a high, thin scream from Ivy Peebles. Then Tom's bull hit the end of the rope, which snapped tight and shuddered with strain. The horse was dragged bodily, his hoofs sliding for several feet, and then the bull went down.

Tom sprang out of his saddle like a cat, a short length of rope in his hand. He covered the distance to the downed bull in seconds, tied the hind legs and drew them up to the head with a loop of rope thrown around the horns where they joined the animal's skull. His horse kept the lariat taut, and the bull lunged and fought against the rope that had made him helpless, all the while bellowing his rage and fear.

Tom looked around. What he saw made ice congeal in his veins. The sound like a pistol shot he had heard had been the parting of Ivy Peebles's cinch. The cinch had snapped under the strain when Ivy's animal hit the end of the rope. Ivy's bull, a white one, was just now struggling to his feet. Ivy was on his knees, gasping to replace the air that had been knocked out of him. His face was ghastly gray with pain, and the bull, seeking about with reddened eyes and lowered head, saw him just as Miguel screamed frantically: "Down, Ivy! Down! If he sees you move, you are dead!"

The bull pawed the ground, snorted, and lowered his head for the charge. A nightmare. Watching, waiting to see a man die, impaled on those lethal, deadly horns. Miguel was too far for the accurate use of his gun, and besides Ivy was between him and the charging bull. And so, frozen, the three of them stood helplessly. The only movement in the clearing was the struggling of the three downed bulls, the thunderous charge of the fourth.

The bull closed the distance between him and the helpless Ivy to thirty feet. Tom realized that he was running, dragging his knife from his pocket as he ran. He cut the rope and the horse side-stepped, but not before Tom had a foot solidly in the stirrup. As the horse whirled away, Tom turned him, using the force thus exerted to lift him and set him solidly in the saddle. Then his great cartwheel spurs dug deeply into the horse's sides. The horse seemed to squat lower against the ground as he surged into a frantic, frightened run. Tom, ten feet behind the bull, could see Ivy's white face and wide eyes.

The horse, coming alongside the bull, veered in close as though he had done this many times before. Leaning widely out of the saddle, Tom seized the bull's tail and dallied it to the saddle horn. As soon as the horse felt its pull, he swerved and set his hoofs. The bull flipped over sideways, hit the ground rolling, and then lay still, his neck broken.

Falling, the bull's body had struck Ivy and knocked him rolling. Now Ivy scrambled to his feet, sweating, trembling violently. He stared at Tom, his eyes dull and glazed with his recent fear.

"I'm obliged," Ivy choked. "I'm mighty obliged."

"Forget it. Skin him out. Hide's worth almost as much as he is."

Three bulls down, a fourth dead. They could be branding four, too, but for a weak and worn-out cinch. Yet they might be branding only three each day henceforth, if Tom had not acted instantly, and Ivy's haunted eyes said he was still aware of this.

Tom dismounted. They gathered wood and Tom built a

fire. They smoked comfortably as they waited for the irons to heat. Miguel, ever the talkative one, murmured almost as though to himself: "Most men stand around and gawk in a moment of crisis. But this one thinks with his hands and body. I believe I am sorry I have promised to teach you to use the gun, for someday you will turn the skill I teach you back upon me."

Tom shrugged. "You can always leave."

Miguel shook his head. "No. I cannot leave. I must stay and do what I have promised to do. I must see you when you come face to face with Schofield. This I cannot help."

Tom grunted, and fished a hot iron out of the fire, an iron that Doc had fashioned last night at his forge. A star. The cross would be made with a bar iron. This work was no stranger to Tom, neither its hazards nor its backbreaking effort. Its rewards, however, were novel. It gave him a feeling of accomplishment he had never known as a boy to see the brand, Star Cross, burned on each animal's hip.

After the branding, they made steers of the bulls and marked their ears with a knife. They squatted around the fire, then, letting the steers grow weak and docile as they struggled futilely against the ropes. Later today, they would release the three and drive them to the corral, but it would not be easy. Most likely, they would have to rope all three of the steers at least once more. A couple of them might need to be thrown two or three times before they became docile enough to drive.

Very occasionally, in extreme cases of stubbornness, it was necessary to get a steer down and sew his eyelids shut with needle and thread, thus blinding him temporarily so that he could not run away. That was a last resort, however, for all its effectiveness.

Tom lay back on the ground and rested.

Beside him, Miguel murmured sleepily: "These first few animals are the hardest, *señor*. But they will grow docile, penned away in a corral. When we release them, they will not be thinking of hiding in the thicket, but only of grass and water to fill their empty bellies. And when they become that way, we can drive the wild ones to them."

Tom grunted. His mind was busy with mental arithmetic. Three or four a day. In a month, almost 100. And when they had 100, it would no longer be necessary to rope each animal they wanted at dawn this way. They would drive to their previously gathered herd and the tamed beasts would absorb the wild ones into their ranks. Then the herd would grow rapidly. By spring, with any luck at all, they could have 400 or 500 head ready for the drive to Indianola where they could be loaded aboard a steamship for the trip to New Orleans.

Tom's mental arithmetic went on. Suppose the 500 brought $10 each. That would be, let's see, $5,000. Was that right? It couldn't be. There wasn't that much money in the world.

Miguel murmured: "*Señor* Cady."

"What?"

"A man should plan. A man must think of the future. What will you do when you are master of a million acres, when your Star Cross brand is upon the flanks of ten thousand cattle?"

"Do?" Tom laughed shortly. "Must a man be different because of the things he owns?"

"Most men are."

Tom shook his head idly, and Miguel sighed. "You are a strange one, *señor*. You care nothing for the land, nothing for the cattle, nothing for the power that money brings. What do you care about?"

Tom raised an elbow, absorbed and intent now. "I care about living and letting live," he said. "Other than that, I care about the smell of the brush when it rains, the new calves in the spring. I want sometimes to lie on my back and watch the clouds pass overhead. I like the cool breeze and the warm ground beneath my body. I like the clean smell of a woman. I. . . ." He stopped, embarrassed. "What do you care about?"

Miguel chuckled. "Enough money so that I need never stop another stagecoach, or walk into another bank with a gun in my hand." He spread his hands. "Other than that, a woman when she pleases me. Enough to drink and a fight when I am angry. That is all, *señor.*"

Tom snorted derisively. "We've branded three steers. It's a long way from that to what you want."

"So we had better get at it." Miguel rose, stretching. He lowered his arms slowly and whispered: "We have company, *señor.*"

Tom got to his feet. Over at the edge of the clearing, two men sat their horses, silently watching. How long they had been there Tom had no way of knowing, but the sight of the big one made his body grow cold and tense. Schofield. The second man had an equally upsetting effect upon Tom. He was the one who had kicked Tom in the head, the one to whom he had made his promise of vengeance.

Schofield touched his horse's ribs with his great, roweled spurs, and rode forward. The other, Ziegler, came behind like a skinny, deadly shadow. They rode to within ten feet of Tom Cady without speaking. Schofield's boar-like eyes were angry, hostile. But Ziegler was smiling, with a watchful kind of pleasure.

Tom stood ready.

Miguel said: "I take it that this is the one who says he will be King of Texas?"

"Schofield," Tom said. "Keep your mouth shut and stay out of this."

"*Si.*" There was no resentment in Miguel, but neither was there agreement.

Schofield said roughly, "I will be King of Texas." He said it with so much certainty that it did not sound absurd.

"You can try, I reckon," Tom said. "But stay out of my way, Schofield. Keep your damned kingdom over where it belongs."

"This is part of it. I claim all this. I claim the steers lying there on the ground. You have no rights here. I bought your father out and paid him five hundred dollars for his land and cattle."

"Not this land," Tom said. "He never owned it."

Schofield ignored him. He turned and threw his voice at Ziegler. "Blot the brands on those three steers. Then cut them loose."

Ziegler started to dismount, on the side away from Tom. Tom was between the pair, with Ziegler on his right, Schofield on his left. Suddenly he snatched the hat from his head and flung it at the head of Schofield's horse. The animal shied from it, and reared. There was a wild kind of fury in Tom as he closed the distance between himself and Schofield. He caught the man's blocky left leg with his hands, braced himself, and yanked. Schofield came tumbling out of the saddle, and the horse spooked fifteen yards before he stopped.

Tom jumped aside, and Schofield hit the ground. Tom kicked him savagely on the side of the head, then stooped and took his gun out of his inert hand. A shot blasted from behind Ziegler's horse, a shot that would have killed Tom Cady if he had not stooped to get Schofield's gun. Coming up, he shot from his crouched-over position.

The bullet took Ziegler's horse in the neck. The animal made a choking, bubbling noise, and collapsed quietly to the ground.

Ziegler looked at Tom, then at Miguel. Miguel was holding a gun on him, too. He dropped his own as if it burned him.

Beside Tom, Schofield was getting up. His mouth looked like a straight, thin, half-healed scar. A wicked promise gleamed in his tiny, boar's eyes. More than ever he reminded Tom of a boar, infuriated beyond all reason and ready to charge. To a boar, what did it matter that death waited at the end of his charge? Tom thumbed back the hammer of the gun with an audible *click*, and his voice came out, rough and insistent and deadly.

"King or not, Schofield, you can die as quick as any man. Now get out of this clearing. Get on back where you belong."

Schofield's battle during the next few moments was with himself. You could tell that in his trembling, ponderous body, in the grim set of his mouth, in the narrowed, tortured eyes. His words came, almost whispered, from between clenched teeth.

"Have you ever put fourteen hours in a coal mine, Cady? Have you ever breathed the dust until your lungs were on fire? Have you ever lived with grime ground into your hide, gritty in your food? Have you ever heard a mule scream at its first sight of sunlight because the pain in its eyes was too great to be borne? I have. From the time I was ten I put fourteen hours a day half a mile underground in a coal mine. I know what it is to be a slave, Cady. I saw my father cough his life away before he was forty. I saw my mother die of overwork, trying to feed herself and me. I'm through being a slave, Cady, and you're in my way. I'll step on you like I would a scorpion. I'm going to be King of Texas, Cady, if I have to kill you and every other living thing that stands in my way. So get out of the country, damn you! Get out, because you're a dead man if you don't!"

Tom heard him out, awed by the very intensity in the man. Then he said: "Maybe so, Schofield, but right now I'm very much alive. So turn around and ride off. Get back on your damned land before I start remembering what you did to me when I first came home."

A vein throbbed and pulsed in Schofield's thick neck. "I'm on my own land. The Big Thicket is mine, from the Gulf all the way to Austin. The cattle in it are mine. You're a rustler, Cady. And you'll hang for one."

Miguel's voice insinuated itself, suave and soft, but somehow sinister. "You have bought four thousand acres, so you claim four million. You have bought a thousand cattle, and you claim half the cattle in Texas. I think I would hate to sell you anything, *señor*. I would not sell you an Army musket, lest you end up as commander in chief of the Army." Miguel laughed tauntingly.

Tom spoke without turning his head. "Shut up, Miguel. Are you trying to make him fight?"

"Why not, *amigo?* Now is as good a time to kill him as any other. Do you tease the rattler and then let him slide away?"

Tom thought that throbbing vein in Schofield's neck would burst. His own throat felt tight, watching it. There was power in Schofield, power that was more than that of force and danger. It seemed almost an inherent thing, as though in spite of his years in the mines, the blood of kings and emperors actually flowed in the big man's veins. It was imperiousness and arrogance, coupled with pitiless cruelty that ordinary men can never match. A clamminess began to spread up Tom's arms. His feet felt numb. But the gun in his hand did not waver. For all Schofield's deadliness, he would die if he moved.

Then the deadliness in Schofield went out of him and he seemed to sag like a bag of grain. "All right, Cady." His voice was even and he almost smiled. "We'll ride out. But nothing is changed, you understand. You're going to die."

Tom didn't answer. Schofield walked over and caught his horse. He mounted, and rode away. Ziegler stared at Tom a moment, smiling. Then he turned and walked after Schofield. In a moment they were lost from sight in the brush.

Tom stuffed Schofield's gun in his belt. Miguel was watching him. Tom said harshly: "Let 'em up. Let's start them toward the corral." He paused, drew in a deep breath. "Tonight I'll belt on that gun and you can give me my first lesson in how to use it."

Miguel smiled. "It will not be difficult, *amigo*. For one who has yet to learn its use, you do very well."

VIII

Immediately upon returning to McGuire's that night, Tom went to his room and strapped on the Colt revolver. He tried drawing it several times, finding himself awkward and slow. A revolver was an unfamiliar weapon in his hand, but instead of giving up, he continued to practice, feeling a little foolish and self-conscious, yet persevering stubbornly.

He kept remembering Schofield's words, spoken with so much determination and certainty: *You're a dead man, Cady.* Sometime, somewhere, a showdown with Schofield awaited him, and the weapons would be revolvers. Therefore, it behooved him to learn the use of this unfamiliar weapon, until his mind was fast as light, his aim unerring as death itself.

Well, he had an expert to teach him. He had better find Miguel right now. He went downstairs and through the kitchen. Hazel was peeling potatoes in a dishpan at the table. He passed her quickly, conscious of the way her eyes went to the gun at his side. She still showed distrust and suspicion, and something approaching dislike. Yet she had negative feelings toward all men, not toward Tom alone, but they were dwindling from day to day, slowly, encouraged to decrease by the apparent lack of interest in her on Tom's part.

Miguel, Ivy Peebles, Polidoro, and Doc were lounging in the yard, awaiting supper. Peebles was idly whittling on a stick. Miguel was cleaning his gun. Polidoro just sat looking at the stars in his cold, preoccupied way.

Miguel saw the gun at once. He said: "Come here, *compañero*. Let me see the holster for a moment."

Tom walked over to him and Miguel slipped the gun in and out of the holster several times. Then he drew a razor-sharp knife from its sheath at his waist and pared carefully at the upper edges of the stiff leather sheath. Finished, he said: "Now, try it."

Tom did. The gun slipped more easily from the holster, and his speed improved considerably.

Miguel said: "Let me have it tonight, *amigo*, after supper. I will get a bar of laundry soap and rub the inside of the holster with it. It slicks the leather without softening it. It is also insurance that the gun will not stick in leather during a rain."

Tom nodded.

Miguel said: "We will use each moment of the day that we can spare for teaching you to use this gun, *señor*. Because it is certain that our friend Schofield will not be patient. He will try to kill you before the week is out and he will go on trying until he succeeds, or until you kill him."

"I've been thinking about that," Tom said. "So starting tomorrow I want a guard out at the corral with the cattle. I want him hidden in the brush with a rifle. I want him to shoot the hell out of anyone that comes around. Ivy, you take it first, tomorrow night. After that, we'll rotate."

He walked off into the brush alone and began to practice drawing the gun. He practiced continuously for the better part of an hour, until the light began to fade and dusk settled down over the land.

Walking back in response to Hazel's call to supper, he felt that he had made some progress. Actually he had made a great deal more progress than he realized, thanks to his natural, instinctive co-ordination of body and mind. Doc McGuire had seen that co-ordination the night of Tom's fight with Stutz. It had fired his imagination and sparked his certainty that an empire could be wrested from the brush if Tom would help.

Supper was a silent meal. Everybody ate steadily with concentration and no talk. Afterward they rose from the table and went out into the night.

Miguel's cigar glowed, making a friendly spot of light in the darkness. Tom thought of old Matt, and wondered again why Matt had died. Could Schofield have had anything to do with it? He wanted to believe Schofield had, yet he also realized how doubtful it was. Schofield's only dealings with Matt had been the purchase of his land and cattle—at a ridiculous price, true, but one that might not have seemed so ridiculous three years ago. $500 he had paid. Tom frowned. What had Matt done with the money? Matt had never been a particularly heavy drinker and his sprees had been short and soon over. Nor had he been a gambler. Could he have been robbed the night he was killed? Tom doubted it. The sheriff had brought Matt down. Certainly no one could have robbed him while he was standing. Was it possible that his attackers had been bent on robbery? Tom shook his head helplessly. He made himself answer this way, just guessing. He needed to know more of the circumstances surrounding Matt's death. He needed to know who the men were who had attacked him.

Suddenly and unaccountably weary, Tom went into the house and went to bed.

Thereafter the days passed uneventfully, with deceptive peacefulness that seemed almost dangerous in itself. They branded cattle in early morning and drove them to the corral, where their herd was slowly growing. Afternoons, Tom and Miguel went off into the brush by themselves, and Tom learned not only to draw the gun swiftly, but to fire it accurately and without sighting.

At first, this was awkward, for always before he had used a rifle, sighted from the shoulder. But gradually he learned that firing a revolver from waist level is just like pointing a finger. Eventually accuracy becomes instinctive.

Nights, one or another of the men would guard the corral, and on this particular night it was Ivy Peebles's turn to stand guard. Ivy watched the dark figures ride away almost wistfully, for he was a gregarious man who hated being alone. He sighed and stared moodily at the dim outlines of the shaggy, long-horned beasts in the corral.

There were twenty now. Some had been gaunted by hunger and thirst. Those caught yesterday and today were ringy and wild. But they would all calm down. Get them hungry enough and thirsty enough, and all they'd want when they were turned out would be grass and water. They'd forget their wildness and their desire to hide in the brush, and grow used to the men who drove them about. They'd absorb other wild ones driven into their ranks. Then it would become easy, and the herd would grow swiftly. Yet with the growth of the herd, so also would the danger from Schofield grow.

Ivy licked his lips and looked out at the brush. The night seemed to stretch away before him endlessly. Tom had said that he could sleep, that if Schofield did come he would make enough noise to rouse a guard. Yet, in spite of that, the night seemed endless and lonely to Ivy. He remembered the first night he had stood guard and all at once he could not stand the prospect of another, similar night alone.

He scowled at the corral and the score of cattle in it. He scoffed aloud: "Hell, Schofield ain't goin' to bother a lousy twenty head of stock. He's going to wait till we got something worthwhile to scatter or steal. He won't come tonight, no matter what Cady says."

Ivy brightened. He started to climb down from the corral, then hesitated. "Where'n hell would I go?" he mumbled. "I can't go to McGuire's, an' it's too damn' far to town."

He licked his lips again. Doc McGuire had a stoneware jug. If he could slip up close to the house and steal Doc's jug, the night wouldn't seem so long. His eyes lighted up. His face became crafty and sly. Better still, why not take tonight and locate Doc's still? If he managed that, he'd have an endless supply of whiskey and no one the wiser.

Ivy climbed down from the fence and went to where his horse was picketed at the end of a long length of rope. He saddled with shaking hands, his throat dry with anticipation of Doc's homemade whiskey. He didn't waste even a backward glance on the corral and its cattle. He rode in a direct line toward Doc McGuire's. Yet in spite of his determination not to let conscience interfere with pleasure, he kept feeling pangs of guilt. He approached Doc's house with extreme caution.

He left his horse a couple of hundred yards away, securely hidden in the brush. Then he stalked ahead on foot. He tried to remember which way Doc went when he headed for his still, but couldn't. Finally he decided that Doc never took a single direction. He always left riding aimlessly, and only took the trail to the still after he was out of sight of the house. How, then, could his trail best be found? Ivy grinned. It was simple, really. All he had to do was to circle the house about a quarter mile from it. He'd pick up Doc's trail soon enough. It would be the one showing the heaviest use.

He began to circle, slinking along through the choking brush like a wolf. From the house he could hear the run of talk as Polidoro and Doc, Miguel and Tom, waited in the yard for the supper call. When he crossed to windward of the house, he could smell frying pork.

Suddenly, ahead of him, he heard a noise. He crouched, seeming to become a part of the choking underbrush. Scarcely breathing, he listened. Two horses coming, Ivy's ears told him. Then the horses were still, and he caught the sounds of two men easing their way stealthily through the brush. Ivy tried to crouch even closer to the ground. He scarcely breathed. The men came closer. He could hear their hoarse panting. It puzzled him, this panting. He raised his head and risked a look.

Then he saw Schofield and Ziegler, each carrying two five-gallon cans of what appeared to be coal oil. The weight of the cans accounted for their shortage of breath. Four big cans of coal oil. They intended to burn Doc's house.

Ivy swallowed to ease the dryness of his throat. Schofield whispered something to Ziegler and they put the cans down on the ground. Then both of them hunkered down to wait.

Ivy understood Schofield's strategy. He had already stirred up enough stink in the country and he didn't want to stir up more by boldly killing either Cady or Doc. But after a house has burned, who can say how the fire began? With his house burned along with all his possessions, would not the heart go out of Doc McGuire? Wouldn't he pull out of this cattle venture, content to have a whole hide?

Ivy thought he would. What Tom would do was another matter. Yet without Doc's support and money to pay the crew, how could Tom carry on alone? Ivy opened his mouth to yell, then closed it abruptly. Long before Tom and the others could get here, Schofield and Ziegler would have done him in. *Get the hell out of here,* a small silent voice told Ivy Peebles. He began crawling on hands and knees through the brush.

It is next to impossible to move noiselessly through the thicket. Even a scorpion will rattle as he moves through the dry leaves. In spite of his caution, Ivy did no better. A twig cracked under his hand. A thorn scratched noisily across his duck brush jacket. Dry leaves crackled under one of his knees.

He heard Schofield's startled voice behind him. He heard the two argue briefly, Ziegler insisting the noise was that of some wild brush creature, Schofield insisting it was not. Had Ivy kept moving, had the noise of his passage continued or even accelerated after they began to speak, doubtless they would have let him go, both believing the noise to have been caused by some wild thing. But he gave himself away by crouching, silent, from the moment they began to talk.

He heard them coming, then, one from the right, one from the left. Wildly for a second, he debated the wisdom of rising and bolting for it, and then it was too late. Brush cracked against him and Schofield's heavy voice said: "Stand up, Ivy."

Ivy stood up. Ziegler came up on the other side of him, forcing his way through the thorny brush. Schofield said softly: "So Cady has put out guards."

Ivy shook his head. "No. Cady doesn't know I'm here."

"Then what are you doing, hiding out in the brush?"

Ivy hesitated. Something about Schofield's expression started his knees to shaking. Schofield's heavy fist lashed out like a mule's hind foot and knocked him sprawling. The thorns of the brush raked his hands as he threw them back to break his fall. He spat blood and struggled to his feet, defiance and anger coming to him at last. "Dammit, all I'm tryin' to do is find Doc's still. I was lookin' for the trail."

"That's better." Schofield chuckled humorlessly. "When I ask you something, answer fast." He paused, and Ivy watched the massive dark figure, barely discernible against the lighter sky. It seemed to grow, to become blacker. "I'll give you a bit of advice, Ivy. Fork your horse and light out for Matadero. Draw your pay from Cady and don't come back."

Stubbornness mingled with fear in Ivy Peebles. He swallowed twice and said defiantly: "Not me, Mister Schofield. Tom saved my neck. He saved me from a bull's horns the first day I worked for him. I ain't quittin' Tom."

Schofield hit him, flat-handed, across the mouth. He said: "Al, see if you can change his mind for him."

Al Ziegler wore his hair long. An uncombed tangle, it

reached almost to his shoulders, and at night it made his sil-
houette look monstrous. Al was a man you'd have branded
harmless unless you looked at his eyes, at his thin, pinched
nose, at his lips, so cruel and pale. If you really looked at
Al, you saw that he was neither harmless nor normal, and
you sensed his abnormality with a shiver you could never
quite repress. Ivy had seen all that, sensed all that in full
daylight. He felt every bit of it now.

Al chuckled. "Leave him to me, Mister Schofield. He'll
leave all right . . . when he's able."

Ivy broke away. He tried to run through the brush, but
the short rope Al was carrying slung over one shoulder
snaked out before he had gone a dozen steps, caught him
around the neck, and brought him down. The rope burned
as it tightened, and then Ivy lay flat, gasping for breath.

He scrambled up frantically, clawed at the rope to loosen
it, then went for his knife. Before he could draw it, Al was
upon him. Al's pistol barrel slashed Ivy's face, leaving its
burning, sticky trail. Al's knee came up and thudded sicken-
ingly against his groin.

Ivy went to his knees. His knife fell, and Al kicked it
away into the brush. Ziegler chuckled softly, thickly.
"Schofield'll want a few broken bones, don't you reckon,
Ivy?"

Ivy screeched as loud as he could.

"Tom! For God's sake . . . !"

Al's boot caught him in the mouth.

Tom had been aware of the sounds in the brush, but because he heard no voices, they seemed usual and harmless.
Ivy's screech brought him instantly to his feet. His hand
went instinctively to his side where the revolver hung.
Then, faintly, he heard Schofield's harsh: "Dammit, Al,
shut him up!"

Tom began to run. From the remoteness of Schofield's voice, he judged that the man was over 100 yards away. Over his shoulder he shouted: "Miguel, watch it here at the house!"

Was this a full-scale attack? And if so, what was Ivy doing out there? Had Schofield jumped the cattle first, and had Ivy come to bring a warning? Brush clawed at Tom, but he made no effort to avoid it. He charged like a bull through the tangle of thorns. Plainly he heard Ivy's whimpering and the dull thudding of boots against a body.

Breaking through a particularly thick tangle of mesquite, he caught a glimpse of Al Ziegler, and somewhere off to the right, a darker shape that must be Schofield. He flung a hasty shot. He saw Ziegler straighten and whirl. He thumbed back the hammer for a second shot, just as Schofield bellowed: "Al! Come on."

Ziegler's shape bobbled as he broke stride, then faded into the brush like a coyote. Tom started to pursue, but he tripped over Ivy's writhing form on the ground, and halted. He knelt beside Ivy, holstering his gun. "Ivy, you all right?"

Ivy groaned. He looked up at Tom, his face bloody and twisted with pain. He gestured weakly with his head. "Coal oil. Over there."

Tom yelled: "Tonio! Doc! Come here!"

He helped Ivy to his feet. Ivy groaned at every movement. Tonio and Doc came pushing through the brush and Tom sent them to get the coal oil. Then he helped Ivy back toward the house.

Ivy began to babble. "They wanted me to quit. I told them no. Then Ziegler. . . ." He broke off and said hysterically: "Help me find my horse, Tom. Get my horse. I've got to get out of here!"

"Later, Ivy. Wait until you feel better. You'll be safe at the house."

"They was goin' to burn it."

"Sure, Ivy, sure. But you stopped them. That was good work." He had seen hysteria cases like Ivy's during the war and he knew just what Ivy needed.

They reached the house. Doc and Polidoro came up carrying the cans of coal oil. Tom picked up Doc's jug from the bench, uncorked it, and handed it to Ivy. Ivy tipped it, choked, and tried again. Tom said: "Take it upstairs with you, Ivy. Drink all you want. We'll talk about this in the morning."

He measured the beaten, frightened man carefully. He didn't underestimate the terror in Ivy, nor his urge to run, but tomorrow both might be less compelling. Despite the beating, Ivy didn't seem to be seriously injured.

Ivy stumbled into the house, and Tom nodded to Miguel. He said: "They're not ready for a showdown. But from here on out we're going to have to guard the house as well as the cattle. And we're going to have to stay together."

IX

Tom turned next to Tonio Polidoro. He surprised the man in the act of staring fixedly at him. A strange one, this Tonio. A good man in the brush, but a strange one, who sometimes looked at Tom as if he hated him. Tom said: "Find Ivy's horse, Tonio, and get out there to the corral. Stay until midnight, and then come back."

"Sí, señor." The words were respectful, but the tone was not.

Frowning, Tom went into the kitchen. Hazel was still

busy preparing supper. Her face betrayed both anger and anxiety.

"Got any coffee?" he said.

"Yes." She got a cup and poured it full. He sat down at the table, and she set it before him. "What happened? Why did they do that to Ivy? He wasn't hurting them."

Tom sipped the scalding coffee. "Ivy left the cattle for some reason, probably to come back here and get a jug. Schofield and Ziegler were skulking around in the brush, waiting until we'd all be asleep. They were going to burn the house. They had twenty gallons of coal oil with them."

Hazel bit her lip and smoothed her apron nervously. The coldness and wariness seemed less in her today, but she was frightened. "Tom, I give it up. I don't want anything that's built on dead men, or ruined lives. Pa is only doing this because of me. I know."

Tom didn't understand his own harshness and impatience. "You're ready now to marry some brush popper and live in a shack? You're ready for the *cantinas* in Matadero? Or have you reconciled yourself to running a roadhouse here in the brush?"

She flushed but said nothing, and Tom was instantly sorry. She'd had little or nothing to do with his decision to fight Schofield.

He got up and stood facing her. "You've forgotten something. I hate Schofield and that skinny shadow of his more than I ever hated the Union Army. I'm going to hurt them the way they hurt me."

A ripple of something akin to pity went over her face. "And when you've done that?"

Tom shrugged.

"I'll tell you, if you don't know. Nothing. Living for vengeance is like drinking to forget anger. When it's over, all that's left is sickness and a bitter taste in your mouth." He didn't say anything, so she went on. "I remember your father, Tom. I remember him well and he wouldn't approve of what you're doing. He may have been a hard man, but he was never vengeful or cruel."

"Then what made him kill five men before they could bring him down?"

She frowned. "I don't know. I wouldn't believe he had, either, if so many people hadn't seen it. But he must have had a reason . . . a good reason."

"I've got a good reason, too."

"Tom, stop it. Already you've changed from the man who rode in here that night half dead. You're harder and colder. You don't care about Ivy Peebles. You think of him as a tool, not as a man, a tool you want to keep so you can defeat Schofield. Ivy hurts tonight, Tom. He hurts the way you did after Schofield got through with you."

She was looking up at him, her eyes shining, her face flushed and earnest. The bodice of her dress rose and fell with her hastened breathing. Tom's arms went out as if they had a will of their own. He had been wanting to do this for a long time. He caught her to him and his lips came down on hers.

She struggled like a caught bird, helplessly. Then she flung her head back and her eyes flamed outrage and indignation. "You're no different from the others," she said in a voice thick with contempt. "You're strong, and can hold me against my will. But you can't stop me from despising you!"

He felt like shaking her. He barely restrained himself. "What's the matter with everyone in this damned thicket?" he said. "They're all so afraid somebody's going to ask something from them. All right. I'm through asking. Now I'm going to take."

This time, his mouth came down hard and bruisingly against hers. And stayed.

Slowly, slowly, the banked fires within her began to burn. Her body tension died and her skin grew hot and moist. Her lips turned soft and her arms went tightly around Cady's corded neck.

He released her and stood before her, panting softly. He grinned. "You're a lot of woman . . . a hell of a lot of woman!"

Her hand cracked like a pistol shot against his cheek. And then she fled, running along the hall and up the stairs. He listened, and heard her angry sobs somewhere in the depths of the house.

He was deeply ashamed. Yet in a way, he was also glad. It took warmth to melt the ice on a pond in spring, and he had started a thaw. No doubt about it. His shame persisted, however, for he knew the kind of warmth Hazel needed was not the kind he had offered her.

Doc came in, with the crew behind him. Seeing Hazel gone, Doc began to dish up supper for himself, and Tom put the girl out of his mind. He had things to do before he would be free to think of her.

He meant to build a herd, build an empire of cattle—a maverick empire. And doing it, he meant to satisfy all the conflicting cravings of his soul—vengeance against Schofield and Ziegler, vindication of Matt through an explanation of his berserk fury, and finally peace within himself. Peace? There would be no peace in the war that lay ahead. Only death, for Schofield, or for Tom, or for both. He could not go back. He could only go on.

Lying awake that night, staring at the ceiling, Tom came to the realization that events were moving toward a rapid and violent climax. For one thing, Schofield's attempt to burn Doc's house, and his decision to intimidate Ivy Peebles instead of making an all-out attack betrayed the fact that Schofield was afraid.

Why, Tom couldn't guess. As yet, Tom and McGuire and their crew constituted no particular threat to Schofield. Their operation, if allowed to continue, would eventually grow from a penny-ante project into one of size and importance. But even so, it would not hurt Schofield. There was enough brush country and enough cattle for both of them, enough, indeed, for a dozen more. Perhaps Schofield's obsession to be King of Texas drove him, making it impossible for him to tolerate competition. Perhaps it was something else. In any event, having committed himself to the extent of trying to burn McGuire out, Schofield would now go further. His next blow would be aimed at the cattle, or directly at the crew.

Tom decided, therefore, that it was time to begin moving fast. Tomorrow, they would release the score of cattle in the brush corral. While one of them held the bunch on a clearing of grass, the others would gather from the brush, driving one, two, or three head at a time to the previously gathered herd.

Next morning, Tom awoke at his accustomed time. Dressing swiftly, he went downstairs to the kitchen. Doc was there, along with Miguel and Tonio Polidoro. Ivy was apparently still abed upstairs. Tom said: "Miguel, today we move. We'll turn the cattle out, and you ride herd on them. Tonio and I will drive to them. Schofield's getting impatient and we need a herd to sell so we'll have the money to hire men and fight him."

"*Bueno, señor.*"

Tom gulped a cup of coffee, then went back upstairs,

carrying a lighted lamp because the morning was still dark. He entered Ivy Peebles's room.

Ivy peered at him out of eyes that were bruised and almost closed. He grinned painfully with his battered mouth. "Time to get up, boss?"

Tom sat down on the edge of the bed. "Not for you, Ivy. I know how you feel, because Schofield gave me the same treatment. You stay in bed today and tomorrow anyway. Then we'll see."

Ivy regarded him with wistful slyness. "Tom, I hurt somethin' terrible. You reckon you could git another of them jugs of Doc's for me?"

Tom grinned. "You'll get one, Ivy. Now go on back to sleep."

Ivy closed his eyes, and Tom went back downstairs. He told Doc to get Ivy a jug, then ate his breakfast quickly.

Hazel acted subdued this morning, and almost furtive. Whenever he looked at her, a rosy flush crept up into her face. He knew that she was ashamed of the response she had showed him last night, and suddenly he felt an unaccountable wave of tenderness for her. She deserved better than what he had offered. She deserved something honest, and decent, and sincere.

Breakfast finished, Polidoro and Miguel went out to get the horses. Tom stayed behind to caution Doc.

"Schofield probably won't come around the house again," he said. "On the other hand, he might figure on us guessing he wouldn't. So keep a sharp lookout. Don't fool around if he comes riding in. Shoot first and ask questions afterward."

Doc nodded nervously. Cady wondered if Doc had the guts for the job.

He needn't have worried, for Hazel said: "I'll watch, too,

Tom. Go on to work, and don't worry. The house will be here when you get back."

Tom nodded, and went out. The change in Hazel was really striking, he thought. She was letting in warmth and shutting out fear. She really meant it about guarding the house. He grinned, feeling better. Schofield had better not come today.

He roped a horse out of the corral and saddled by lantern light. Then, blowing out the lantern and hanging it on the corral, he mounted and led out.

They covered the distance to the brush corral in a little more than an hour, arriving just as dawn streaked the sky. They found the cattle still inside, although restive and bellowing with hunger and thirst. Cady let down the bars, and they drove the docile cattle out and headed them toward a nearby clearing. Here the cattle bunched, grazing with famished concentration. Miguel grinned at Tom. "*Bueno, compañero.* They will not be hard to hold. Get us some wild ones, something to make this game worthwhile."

Tom nodded. He noticed Tonio staring at him in his odd way, and was momentarily disturbed by it. Tonio moved away, and Miguel said softly: "*Un momento, señor.*"

Tom waited.

Miguel said: "Who is that one? And why does he hate you so?"

"Hate me? Hell, I never saw him before in my life until the day Doc hired him."

"He knows you, *amigo.* And he hates you. Remember it when you are out in the brush with him alone."

Tonio had turned. Now he was staring back at them. Tom spurred toward him.

Miguel's words had a disturbing effect, exaggerated though this seemed to be. Tom had noticed the way Tonio looked at him often enough, and had wondered about it more than a little bit. Now, he put it out of his mind. He led away, and before he had gone 1,000 yards he spotted a bull and two young cows spooking away through the brush.

Uttering a high yell, Tom set his spurs. The brush-wise horse, seeing the cattle himself, dug in his hoofs and began to run. A wild thrill of exultation possessed Tom. The mesquite, the black chaparral clutched at him. At times he was forced to throw his body sideways, clinging to the neck and back of his horse. Always he kept his eyes open, for to close them even an instant could mean being swept from the saddle.

The horse dodged, anticipating the movements of the fleeing cattle. Tom could hear Tonio, riding on his right, by the crashing his horse made tearing through the brush. Slowly they gained on the trio. As they gained, Tom forged ahead and began to turn the cattle while Tonio fell behind slightly to allow them room to turn.

Tom guessed they had gone almost two miles before he got the cattle turned. He pointed them back in the direction they had come, guided now only by his brush popper's uncanny directional sense. If a man didn't have it, he was lost. Aiming this way through the brush tangle, even a slight miscalculation meant that he missed the clearing at which he aimed. And if he missed, he never got a second chance, for the cattle would be gone.

Tom did not miss. A few moments later he and Tonio burst out of the thicket twenty yards behind the fleeing cattle. They split at once, riding out to right and left of the three, thus heading them directly at the grazing bunch. Miguel had prudently disappeared, but Tom knew he was hidden on the other side of the clearing, prepared to turn the cattle if they showed signs of trying to break away.

They had been run far enough, however, to be glad to stop. They entered the grazing herd, creating scarcely a stir, and stood dispiritedly with heads hanging and tongues lolling out.

Miguel came from the brush and waved. Tom and Tonio whirled and returned to search for more.

This way, the morning passed. Time and again, Tom and Polidoro returned to the clearing, driving before them one to half a dozen head. By mid-afternoon they had doubled their herd of twenty.

"That's enough!" Tom called to the others. "Take them back to the corral. By the time we get these branded, it'll be dark."

The herd was restive, holding as it did so many wild ones. But, by hard riding that disregarded the continuous threat of death or disablement, the crew put the herd through the brush and back to the corral from which they had started.

In them all now, a strong feeling of accomplishment was growing. They built up a fire and began to heat their irons. After that, Miguel and Tom entered the corral, while Tonio tended the branding irons.

Tom would rope one around the horns, while Miguel put his rope on the animal's two hind legs. Then, by pulling against each other, the two horses would stretch out the bull and dump him to the ground, bellowing helplessly.

Tonio would come rushing in, with iron and knife, and before he left would throw off the loop around the hind legs. When he was clear, Tom would release the animal by a dexterous flip of the wrist that lifted his loop clear of the horns.

They rode home at dark, Tonio and Tom, having left Miguel at the corral as guard. Although scratched and bleeding in a dozen places, Tom was exuberant. Yet he could not forget, riding along with Tonio behind him, the warning Miguel had given him. Nor could he forget Schofield. The man would be wild when he discovered how well Tom was doing. Perhaps he'd be wild enough to move hastily and foolishly. Tom could only hope that he would. A hasty, angry Schofield, could be beaten. A crafty careful Schofield could not. It was as simple as that.

X

Tom saw the buggy immediately as he rode out of the thicket and into McGuire's clearing. He reined in beside it and studied it in the faint lamplight cast from the windows of the house. Its once shiny paint was now scarred by brush, caked with mud and dust. Its top hung in shreds. Yet upon its side the words **AUSTIN LIVERY STABLE, NO. 37** were still visible.

Tom frowned, puzzled. The main road from Austin to Matadero ran several miles to the west. It seemed unlikely that any through traveler could have wandered this far from the road, and why would anybody hire a rig in Austin and drive to Matadero through the thicket? It would be much easier to ride one of the weekly stages. Still, the thing was here. Someone had driven it from Austin.

Two saddles lay on the ground nearby, so Tom guessed two riders had accompanied the buggy. He rubbed his chin thoughtfully. The driver of the buggy must be a person of importance who had expected some danger during the course of his journey, else why the guards? Tonio had disappeared in the direction of the corral. Tom followed him and released his weary horse.

He slung his saddle to the top pole of the corral and buckled the cinch around a lower pole to hold it in place. Then he strode toward the house. He had never seen lamplight burning in the front of the house, but he did tonight. His curiosity increased.

Doc McGuire was not in his accustomed place beside the back door, nor was Hazel in the kitchen. The odor of roasting pork wafted a tantalizing welcome to Tom, however, so he shed his brush jacket and sank into a chair at the table.

Hazel came into the kitchen, flushed with excitement. She opened the oven door and peered at her roast and baking bread.

"Who's your company?" Tom asked.

She smiled, pleased by the change of routine the company had provided. "Folks from the East," she said breathlessly. "A man and his daughter who lost the road to Matadero. They're spending the night with us." She halted beside his chair. "Tom, it's wonderful to see someone from . . . well, from some place else. You ought to see her clothes."

Tom nodded. There was no envy in Hazel, but only a pleased, almost child-like excitement. She deserved nice things herself, and, if this cattle thing worked out, by God, he intended for her to have them.

"How's Ivy?" he asked.

At once she sobered. "He's scared half to death, Tom. He wants to leave as soon as he can travel."

"Is he still pretty sick?"

"He keeps himself half unconscious with Pa's whiskey. But he hurts, Tom. His face twists up every time he moves."

"I'll go up and see him."

"Wait until after supper. He's asleep now. Come in and meet our guests."

Tom rubbed his whiskered face ruefully, then followed her down a long hall and into a large parlor that was not, however, the largest or most ornate one in the house. A couple of lamps were burning, lamps with colored glass shades. He saw Doc in a far corner of the room, engaged in earnest conversation with another man, a stranger, and across the room from them was the most beautiful woman he had ever seen.

Sitting in the shadows behind McGuire and the stranger were two other men, neither entering the conversation nor pointedly avoiding it. Tom studied them briefly. They were not natives. Apparently they had accompanied the older man and his daughter from wherever they came in the East. Tom's interest mounted.

Hazel said: "Miss Bassett, Mister Bassett, this is Tom Cady."

Tom bowed to the girl. Bassett, a graying man of perhaps sixty with goatee beard and small mustache, rose and extended his hand. Tom took it. Bassett's eyes were very blue and very intent.

Hazel did not introduce the other two men.

Tom sat down on a dusty brocade sofa, suddenly very conscious of his work-weary and soiled appearance. He knew his face was scratched in half a dozen places, and his beard was two days old. In spite of that, he found the girl watching him, and therefore gave his attention to her. She could not have been any older than Hazel, although her manner was considerably more assured. She smiled at him with her full, pleasant mouth and dark brown eyes. Covertly he studied the delicious curve of the bodice of her dress, which was of some heavy silk material.

Her voice was soft, almost intimate. "You fought in the Rebellion, Mister Cady?"

He grinned at her. "Your choice of words is poor for this part of the country, Miss Bassett. I fought in the War Between the States."

"Of course. I'm sorry."

Doc McGuire and Bassett kept on talking in low-voiced, earnest tones, but try as he would Tom could not overhear enough of it to get the gist of their conversation. He did, however, gain the impression that Bassett was asking questions and McGuire answering them. And once he heard McGuire say—"De Chelly . . ." and immediately afterward—"Durand."

Hazel left the room, probably to supervise her dinner. In her absence, Tom found the conversation of Miss Bassett fascinating. She was from Washington, it appeared, and her name was Annemarie. She thought that Texas, and particularly this part of it, was as near to hell as a person would ever get on earth.

Tom said: "You have to be born a Texan to like it, Miss Bassett. Besides, it was a lot better place to live in before all the Yankees moved in."

She flushed prettily at that, and apologized for her remarks. Tom found himself liking her in spite of her inept way of saying the wrong thing. Also, he was flattered by her obvious interest in him. She was a type of woman strange to him, soft, pale, and helpless. Tom was used to strong-bodied Texas women who could work like a man and often did—women like Hazel.

Hazel returned, glanced at Tom, then in a rather sharp voice announced dinner. She preceded them into the huge dining room, which seemed to have been hastily dusted for the occasion. Annemarie put her hand lightly on Tom's arm and walked with him to the dining room. Hazel frowned at them. She went out, and a moment later Tonio Polidoro came in, shuffling along in his straw sandals, and took a place next to one of Bassett's guards.

Hazel carried in the roast, a huge tureen of potatoes, and another of gravy. Tom, deep in conversation with Annemarie, scarcely noticed Hazel, but he did overhear Doc saying: "We're building what you might call a maverick empire here, Mister Bassett. During the four years of war, all the able-bodied men in Texas were gone. Cattle just didn't get branded and taken care of like they should, particularly in the thicket where it's so much harder to do than it is anywhere else. Consequently the thicket is filled with cattle that wear no brand. Mavericks, we call 'em. They belong to the man who can put his iron on their hides."

Bassett expressed polite interest.

Doc asked bluntly: "What's your business here, Mr. Bassett? Cattle?"

Bassett hesitated noticeably. "You might say it was cattle. I hope to buy some beef for the states on the Eastern seaboard."

"Good! Good!" Doc said. "Texas can use hard cash these days. It's one thing we ain't got. That damned De Chelly keeps us milked dry with his exorbitant taxes. I'd bet the gov'ment in Washington don't see more'n a third of the money, either. I'd bet it all goes into De Chelly's pocket."

The statement seemed to interest Bassett, and, thereafter, Doc and he carried on a conversation in undertones.

Hazel listened with only part of her mind. Mostly she covertly watched the vivacious, assured Annemarie Bassett and Tom Cady. It angered her, the way Tom was so obviously attracted to the girl. And yet, she wondered, why should it anger her? Tom's life was his own, to do with as he chose. He meant nothing to her. If he wanted to make a fool of himself over this girl, that was his business. And he *was* making a fool of himself. Annemarie cared nothing for him. She was simply making the best of a dull evening, no doubt one of many on her long journey, with the most attractive man available.

Hazel got up and began to clear the table, but no one seemed to notice her. She carried the dishes to the kitchen and stacked them on the table. Annemarie did not offer to help.

Washing them in the kitchen, Hazel examined her feelings ruefully. The truth was, she liked Tom Cady very much, and tonight she was jealous. She remembered the day he had kissed her, remembering with an overly warm face the way she had responded to him. Yet the kiss itself had been brutal, the same sort of kiss she'd fought away from a dozen times and with a dozen different men. The others she had hated for their crudeness. Tom she did not hate. Why? She asked herself the question, but found no answer. She told herself once more that all men were alike. They seemed to have just one thing on their minds, and they all thought a girl should throw herself into their arms.

Hazel smiled to herself, ridiculing her own bitterness. It was not like that. She must never admit it was like that. Of course, some men were interested only in taking whatever they could get from a girl, but there had to be another kind, the kind capable of deep and lasting love, of giving as well as taking. The whole concept of marriage was built on that kind of relationship. Perhaps men were just animals until they loved a woman. Perhaps then they changed.

She allowed herself to wonder what it might be like, married to Tom Cady. Then she made herself stop it. She didn't want Tom. He was like all the rest of the men in the brush country. He'd build her a one-room shack some-where out in the brush and there they'd stay. She'd raise half a dozen kids and with each one would lose a little more of her youth. In the end, she'd have nothing.

Then what did she want? Money? She shook her head. No, she was not interested in money for itself, or even for the things it would buy. Only security interested her, just knowing that hunger would never trouble her, just being sure that she would never have to go into the *cantinas* in Matadero, or marry solely for a roof over her head and food in her stomach. Was everyone that worried about security? Or was it only she?

Her nervous fingers dropped a dish and it shattered on the floor. And suddenly Hazel began to cry. She left the kitchen and went out into the night. Here she admitted that she both hated and envied Annemarie Bassett, who could in a single evening so completely capture Tom Cady. And she thought frantically: *Tom look out! She'll hurt you. She's just amusing herself.* But Tom would not look out. He was blind, as all men were. Or was he? Could it not be that, com-pletely honest himself, he simply believed others to be just as honest?

Hazel wiped away her tears, and with a still, expression-less face returned to the kitchen. Momentarily forgetting Annemarie, she thought about Tom alone, about his hatred of Schofield and his bitter disillusionment over the way his father had died, and she came to realization that Tom needed help more than he needed anything else—help that she might give if she would try. Help before it was too late, before hatred destroyed him or Schofield killed him.

She carried a plate up to Ivy Peebles and talked with him for a while. When she came down, the house was dark, and everyone had gone to bed. She went to her room and undressed. Somewhere, perhaps in the town of Matadero, lay the answer to Matt Cady's berserk fury and subsequent death. Tomorrow, she would go there. She could ride with the Bassetts in their buggy.

First she would see Sheriff Durand. He was the one who had brought Matt Cady down. After that, she would see whoever she had to see. But somewhere she would find the answer. With her mind made up, and with inaction over and a course decided upon, Hazel slept soundly and peacefully.

She awoke before daylight, hearing Tom Cady's voice in Ivy Peebles's room. She dressed swiftly, went downstairs, and began to prepare breakfast. Tonio Polidoro came in and sat silently at the table, waiting.

After a while Tom came down, and then Miguel. They sat down with Tonio.

Tom said: "No trouble last night, Miguel?"

"None, señor." Miguel's expression was oddly mocking. "But a strange thing happened this morning as I was returning. I found some hogs rooting at a spot in the brush not far from this house."

"Where?" Tom asked sharply.

Miguel launched into a description of the place, meanwhile watching Tom with careful eyes. As he talked, Tom's face seemed to relax almost imperceptibly.

"The strange thing about these rooting hogs," Miguel said, "is that they had rooted out a spot almost the exact size and shape of a grave."

Tom laughed. "Miguel, you're a liar. What's the matter? Do you think I had something to do with Stutz's disappearance? Do you think Stutz is dead? I think you're wrong all the way around. In the first place, Stutz left here alive. In the second, I don't even think he's dead. Likely he'd made all he figured it was safe to make and skipped the country."

Miguel shrugged. "Is possible, *amigo*. It is also possible that I described the wrong place to you, is it not?"

Tom grinned deliberately at him. "You figure that one out, my friend. In the meantime, we've got work to do."

Hazel studied Tom's face as he got up to go. It was filmed lightly with sweat. If Miguel had not caught that expression of intense relief, Hazel had.

She went to the door and watched them tramp across the dark yard toward the corral. Was it possible that Cady had, indeed, killed Stutz? Or that her father had? However she hated to admit it, guilt could be the only reason for Cady's discomfiture. Then he was in trouble, serious trouble. Not only was Schofield after him to kill him, but soon the law would be after him as well.

For a moment, panic ran unchecked through Hazel. She started to run out into the yard, but halted, knowing the hopelessness of it. No, she had to do this another way, and she must be careful, very careful.

Her father came into the kitchen, followed by the Bassetts. While the two guards went out to harness and saddle, Hazel set their breakfast on the table. Leaving them to eat, she ran to her room to dress for town.

She selected her best dress, one made from new material and not from old draperies. Then she went downstairs to wait until the Bassetts would be ready to go.

XI

The ride to town was stiff and painful for both Hazel and Annemarie. They were polite to each other, but beneath their politeness lurked the sharpness of mutually acknowledged dislike. Hazel sighed with relief when the buggy drew to a halt beside the plaza to permit her to alight.

Matadero, like so many Spanish towns, was built around the central plaza or square. From it the streets radiated like the spokes of a wheel. All the important buildings fronted on the plaza and all were adobe. On one side was the courthouse that also housed the sheriff's office and jail. The remainder of it had been commandeered by Union troops as headquarters and billets for the men.

Directly across the plaza was the San Rafael Mission, its twin towers rising highest of all the buildings in town. On the two remaining sides of the plaza were high-walled houses, a livery stable, the Alamo Hotel, and several *cantinas*. The plaza itself was bare, dusty ground, surrounded by a cobbled walk. In the center was a wooden bandstand, where on some nights a band played accompaniment to the promenade of people strolling on the cobbled walk.

Bassett jumped down and helped Hazel to the ground. "We are in your debt for putting us up last night. Thank you very much."

Annemarie added her thanks to those of her father's. Then Bassett got back in and the buggy drove away, followed by the two silent outriders. Hazel hesitated for a moment, feeling small and alone and uncertain. She had no clear idea of how to go about learning more of the facts surrounding Matt Cady's death, other than just to go into Durand's office and ask questions. What compulsions had driven Matt? Had he been drinking? Was he worried about Tom fighting the war in Georgia? What were the names of the men he had killed?

Hazel lifted her skirt clear of the ground and walked across the dirty street. She came into the shade of the gallery and headed toward Sheriff Durand's office. Two or three doors down, she saw the blue-clad form of Major De Chelly. He was staring at her with peculiar intensity.

She went quickly inside the sheriff's office, and was immediately stricken by the stench from the jail cells at the rear. Back there, a soft voice was praying in Spanish. Durand sat with his feet on his desk, snoring softly, his leonine head lolling forward upon his chest. Hazel sat down to wait.

She had been waiting less than five minutes when she sensed a presence in the doorway behind her. A voice, one familiar to her because of the incident in the yard several nights before, said with its Yankee, Down-East twang: "Ma'am, you shouldn't have to wait on him. Want me to wake the old fool?"

She turned. De Chelly's lips were smiling and his eyes were hot and bold.

He was a tall, stooped man, lean and spare except for the slight rounded paunch under his belt. He turned from her to Durand and said harshly: "Durand! Hey! Come out of it! You've got a visitor!"

The snoring stopped. Durand stirred and woke up. Immediately his feet came off the desk. There was a light film of sweat on his deep-lined face, a surprised, startled blankness in his eyes. "Oh. It's you."

The major said peremptorily: "Present me, Durand."

Durand stood up. "Miss McGuire, Major De Chelly."

Hazel nodded coldly. De Chelly's smile grew sardonic with his recognition of her name, and a certain eagerness came into his manner.

Angered, Hazel said: "I want to talk to you, Mister Durand. Privately." She could guess De Chelly's reactions upon meeting Doc McGuire's daughter. He was thinking that her principles were probably no better than Doc's. He was thinking that she would be an easy conquest.

Durand said—"Sure, Miss McGuire."—but he didn't ask De Chelly to leave.

Hazel put a direct stare on the major. A gradual, slow flush crept up into his face. Abruptly he turned on his heel and strode out.

The sheriff laughed uncomfortably. He spoke in a low voice. "I got to play along with 'em, ma'am, but, by God, I don't have to like it. What's on your mind? Somethin' about Roy Stutz?"

Hazel shook her head. "No. But I'm worried about Tom. I was wondering how much you knew about the way his father died."

The sheriff's face was lined, genial, dark-tanned, his eyes almost black. There was no perceptible change in his expression, yet Hazel had the impression that it froze for the barest instant.

He fished in his pocket for a cigar. "Only what everybody knows, I reckon. He raised pure hell for about ten minutes. Killed five men and wounded half a dozen besides."

"Was he drinking? What made him do it?"

"He was drinkin', sure enough." The sheriff struck a match and touched the flame to the end of a long, black cigar.

Hazel felt as if a door had closed and locked in her face. "Can't you tell me what happened?"

"Why?"

She spoke with quick asperity. "Because I'm worried about Tom, that's why. Because I'd like to know. . . ."

"You afraid Tom might turn out like Matt did?"

"Of course not. But. . . ." She faltered, thinking of Stutz, who had disappeared, and who she was sure Tom had killed. She thought of Schofield and Ziegler, and Tom's suppressed savagery when he spoke of them. Confused, she tried to resume talking, but couldn't.

"Might have been the heat," Durand said finally. "That was a hot summer. Might have been worry about Tom an' the war. Anyhow, Matt come to town one day and got himself all likkered up. He was over there at the Fighting Cock." Durand gestured out the open door toward one of the *cantinas* across the plaza. "He got himself in a fuss with some men at the bar. Asked 'em outside. Fought with his fists a little while first, and then all of a sudden he drawed his gun an' commenced shootin'." Durand shrugged. "That's about all there is to it."

"Who finally shot him down?"

"I did." Durand cleared his throat twice. "I was charged with keepin' the peace, you understand. I had no choice."

Hazel nibbled her lip, unwilling, unable to give up. Durand's account had been straightforward, and apparently without subterfuge. Yet she could not shake the feeling that something was being withheld.

She asked: "Who were the men he killed?"

Durand sighed. "That's been three years ago, Miss McGuire. It's a matter of public record if you think it's important enough."

"You mean to say you don't remember any of their names? Five men are killed in one day and you don't remember their names?"

Durand colored slowly. He said irritably: "I'm a busy man, Miss McGuire. Now why don't you just run along and . . . ?"

"You weren't busy when I came in, Sheriff."

Durand inspected the ash on his cigar. "All right. All

right. Mebbe I could remember 'em if I tried." He frowned. "Lessee, there was Sam Hodges, an' Howie Peale, an' Stu Every." He chewed the cigar pensively. "Other two was Mexicans. Federigo Feliz an' Ambrosio Polidoro."

"And the wounded?" Excitement was stirring in Hazel.

"Like I said, it's been a long time. I don't remember the wounded."

"Your memory turned out to be good enough on the ones he killed."

Durand's black eyes were getting progressively harder. He said: "You trying to make somethin' out of this?"

Hazel shook her head. "I'm sorry, Mister Durand. But tell me one more thing. How did he kill and wound so many? Surely no gun holds that many bullets."

"Uhn-huh. They don't. He took a gun from one of the men he killed, an', when that was empty, he drawed his knife."

Hazel stood up. "Thanks for telling me."

Relief eased the sheriff's brown-lined Indian face. His geniality returned, like the sun coming from behind the clouds. "You're sure welcome, Miss McGuire. Any time."

Hazel stepped out onto the gallery. The sheriff's voice followed her. "He was crazy, Miss McGuire. It was just that an' nothin' more."

She whirled suddenly. "Those names, Sheriff. I don't recognize any of them as names I've heard before. What were they doing here? Who were they working for?"

The sheriff opened his mouth automatically. He said: "Scho. . . ." And then shut it like a trap. Hazel said— "Thank you, Sheriff."—and turned away.

For a moment, she stood at the edge of the gallery, looking out into the hot, sun-washed street. Few people were abroad in Matadero during this *siesta* hour. A mangy dog across the street sat up and scratched idly at a flea behind his ear. A small, brilliantly plumaged rooster wriggled luxuriously in a deep dust puddle. Horses at the tie rail switched their tails at flies and drowsed.

So the men Matt had killed had been working for Schofield? And that one—Polidoro. An unusual name, particularly notable when it turned up twice in the same locality, once among men killed by his father, and again among men hired by the son. The whole thing was beginning to look. . . . Hazel shook her head, and some inner wisdom cautioned: *Don't tell Tom yet. Don't tell him until you're sure.*

She heard a step on the walk behind her, heard the smooth voice of Major De Chelly. "A hot day, Miss McGuire. Would you like a cold drink?"

Hazel turned. Her instincts rebelled at going anywhere with this soft, white, oily-mannered man. She didn't trust him. He made her skin crawl. Yet something touchy and defensive in De Chelly's face made her withhold both scorn and refusal. White and soft he might be. He was also powerful, and a bad man to make an enemy of. He commanded the troops that were absolute law in this country just now. And then there was Stutz. If she angered De Chelly, he might, out of balked fury, try to pin Stutz's disappearance either on Tom or upon her father.

She made herself smile, and Major De Chelly, gracious now, bowed and smiled in return. He held out a crooked elbow, and Hazel took it. Together they headed along the shaded gallery toward the Alamo Hotel.

They walked into the lobby. In spite of herself, Hazel felt a sudden tingle of pleasure. The lobby was a monstrous, high-ceilinged room, furnished with rich leather cushions. Tapestries brightened the walls, and a dozen potted palms made the vast expanse seem cool and restful. Double doors opened off to the right into the hotel bar. The dining room was on the left, across the lobby. Major De Chelly walked toward it.

A quiet, leisurely, gracious place. A place of white linen-covered tables, of soft-spoken, white-garbed Negro waiters. The major led her to a table and held her chair gallantly. Save for two elderly Spanish men quietly conversing in a far corner, they were alone.

Hazel ordered lemonade, the major whiskey and water. When the waiter had gone away, De Chelly reached across the table and took one of Hazel's hands in both of his own. His palms were damp and soft. He squeezed her hand. "You're too lovely a woman to be wasted out in the brush country," he said.

Hazel colored slightly. She smoothed the pure white tablecloth with her free hand, then stopped lest she appear nervous.

"Don't you hate the loneliness?" De Chelly asked. "Don't you miss the excitement and pleasures of town living?"

"How could I miss them? I never had them."

"Then tonight you shall! We'll dine here at the hotel, and dance afterward in the *cantinas* on Calle El Centro. We'll walk in the plaza and listen to the band. I'll show you what you miss, living in the Big Thicket."

His eyes were lighted with enthusiasm, his face taut with excitement, and she could see what he really was thinking of—afterward, the long night, when the festivities would be done.

The waiter brought the lemonade. Hazel sipped it slowly, panic rising in her heart. She should have refused him back there on the gallery before the sheriff's office. She

107

should refuse him now. But there was Stutz, who Tom had killed. There was this Yankee's incredible power that could convict a man without a shred of evidence against him, or have him killed outright. Slowly, with a certain hopelessness, Hazel nodded her head. She smiled up into De Chelly's oily face, and tried to deny her fear.

That afternoon he took her on a tour of the town, and of the military installation. Hazel saw De Chelly's prison, with which he had threatened Tom Cady that night in McGuire's yard. It was the old Spanish dungeon, forty feet below ground level and dark and damp as a tomb. Rats scurried away before their approach along the moldy corridors. Men whimpered like animals at the sight of the light, or screamed imprecations at De Chelly and the guards.

As to the purpose of the tour, Hazel could not be sure, but she could guess. De Chelly was making a threat, a promise. By sly indirection, he was saying: *Be nice to me, my dear, or your precious father and that damned Tom Cady will rot in one of these verminous cells.*

When night came, Hazel and Major De Chelly entered the huge dining room of the Alamo Hotel and ran a gauntlet of stares. Without exception, the stares of the men were admiring. Also, without exception, the stares of the women were hostile. Some were obviously envious. Some were contemptuous, plainly condemning her for her association with De Chelly.

De Chelly held her chair while she sat down, his pasty complexion mottled with the fever of expectancy. He could scarcely take his eyes from her. And, indeed, she made a striking picture in the soft lamp glow, with her gleaming midnight hair, done tonight in a bun low on her neck, with her flawless ivory skin, with her eyes as green as bayou water on a bright day. Her lips were a splash of scarlet, her cheeks flushed with what might have been excitement but was in reality fear.

All during dinner, De Chelly sought to dazzle her with talk of the North, of New York, Boston, and Philadelphia. She replied with smiles and polite phrases, and attacked her dinner hungrily in spite of her fear. De Chelly kept drinking wine, scarcely touching his food.

At last the meal was over and De Chelly was standing up. "Are you ready to go, my dear?" His smile was fatuous, fixed. Hazel wondered if his thoughts were as obvious to others in the room as they were to her.

From the hotel they turned right toward Calle El Centro. Half a block from the hotel, and before they had left the plaza, De Chelly drew Hazel into a doorway. He was surprisingly strong for one who appeared so soft. She felt his arms go about her, felt herself drawn close against him. His lips sought hers, hot and eager.

"No," she whispered. "No, please!"

He laughed confidently. Holding her with one arm, he fumbled at the door with the other. Hazel suddenly realized where they stood—at the doorway to his quarters. Wild rage possessed her, rage that turned her face bloodless, that set her body to shaking. She struggled frantically, but De Chelly had both arms free now, and her struggles were useless and futile. Hazel uttered a sharp cry and sank her teeth into his arm.

With a curse, he struck her across the mouth. He flung her through the doorway, followed, and slammed the door behind. In utter darkness, Hazel struggled to her knees. She could hear his heavy breathing as he advanced toward her. His voice was throaty with frustration and insane rage. "Damn you, I'll let Cady and your old man rot in that prison you saw this afternoon!"

Hazel's whole body shook uncontrollably. Her throat closed. She couldn't even scream. She managed to stand up. She felt trapped, like an animal. She retreated to the far wall and he came after her, mouthing obscenities in his hoarse, panting voice. He tripped on a chair and fell heavily to the floor.

Shaking off the paralysis of stark terror, she turned and fled, flinging wide the heavy front door and stumbling as she went through it onto the gallery. Then, as fast as she could go, she ran along it until she came to a dark side street. She ducked into it. She ran until her breath was gone, until she could run no more.

She had to get home, somehow, and quickly. Both her father and Tom Cady must get out of the country at once. If they did not, they were lost.

XII

Tom watched the Bassetts' buggy drive away toward Matadero, then turned toward the corral and the horses that Miguel and Tonio had caught and saddled.

Doc sat down on the bench beside the door with his rifle. Tom was already mounted when he saw Ivy Peebles come unsteadily out of the back door.

Ivy shouted tipsily: "Saddle one for me, boys! I've had enough of that bed."

Tom chuckled. Ivy may have gotten his courage out of one of Doc's jugs, but regardless of the source it had returned. He waited until Ivy mounted, then rode into the brush with the others stringing out behind.

When they arrived at the corral, Tom put Ivy to holding the gathered herd, while he, Tonio, and Miguel worked the brush. Thereafter, they rode all day at a breakneck pace through the thorny brush, driving wild cattle to the now tame herd that grazed, loosely held, in one clearing after another. The herd absorbed the ladinos, gave them a feeling of security, and kept them from breaking wildly back into the brush.

At sundown, Tom and Miguel, Ivy and Polidoro, sweating and grimed, bleeding from countless brush scratches on face and hands, pushed the entire herd back into the strong brush corral.

Miguel grinned at Tom. "I tally eighty-two. I will stay here again tonight, *amigo*, to guard them. Over half are not even branded and I would hate to see them lost."

Tom nodded and rode away, with Tonio and Ivy close behind.

In early dusk, he rode into McGuire's clearing. Hazel had not returned. Ivy volunteered to prepare supper, and, while he did, Tom rode a circle in the brush searching for fresh tracks. He did not intend that Schofield and Ziegler should catch them unaware again. He rode without haste, although the light was fading fast. He wanted to make sure of every yard of ground.

Swinging to the right, he almost encircled the house before he cut sign. He reined his horse about and followed the tracks. A single horseman had left them, and, because they were not deeply indented, Tom judged that they had been made by a light-weight rider rather than a heavy one. Ziegler then. But what the hell was he up to now?

The tracks came out on the road. There they mingled with a profusion of prints, scuffed and sometimes overlying one another. Then they went away into the brush and stopped again. Something about the tracks back there on the road bothered Tom Cady. He thought it over, and then he knew what it was. He spurred away on Ziegler's trail. The wheel prints of the buggy had overlaid the Ziegler horse's hoof prints in the dust of the road—which meant he had been here this morning when the buggy left. He had ridden into the brush when he heard it coming, and waited until it passed.

Still reading sign, Cady came into the road again half a mile from the house. Here he saw what he'd feared he'd see—Ziegler's tracks falling in behind the buggy as it made its way toward town. Alarm stirred in Tom. Schofield had tried threats and intimidation. He'd tried to burn the house. Wasn't it possible that he'd now try to get at Tom and McGuire through Hazel?

Tom whirled his horse and raced back toward McGuire's. He reined in to a walk before he reached the clearing. No sense alarming Doc and Ivy. They'd be needed to watch the house while he and Tonio rode to town.

He found Tonio at the corral, tall, almost wraith-like, his thin, ascetic face with its faintly protruding front teeth barely visible in the deepening dusk light. Tom said hastily: "Catch yourself a fresh horse, Tonio. We're going to town. Somebody was hanging around here this morning and followed the Bassetts' buggy to town."

"Schofield, señor?"

"More likely Ziegler."

Tom caught himself a fresh horse and saddled quickly while Tonio did likewise. As they rode out, Tonio said: "Do not alarm yourself, señor. Perhaps the rider was neither Schofield nor Ziegler. Perhaps he is following the man Bassett, and the reason Bassett must hire guards to ride with him."

Cady spurred his horse to a run. He had to admit that Tonio might be right, but somehow did not believe he was.

No. It made more sense to assume that Schofield planned to attack them through Hazel, having failed in other ways. If she disappeared, Doc would pull out of the deal, and, if Doc pulled out, Tom would have no choice but to pull out, too.

Tom Cady crowded his horse into an even faster pace. Behind him, Tonio had all he could do to keep up. The hours and miles passed beneath his horse's hoofs with maddening slowness. Hazel had been gone more than twelve hours. It was probably already too late. Tom kept remembering Ziegler, recalling the man's obvious abnormality. What would he do to Hazel? Tom felt cold, wondering about that.

Halfway to town he reined his horse to a halt, dismounted, and began to rub the animal down briskly. Tonio followed suit. Thereafter, Tom walked the horse for about a mile to cool him out. Then into the gallop again. At nine they rode through the outskirts of Matadero.

A band was playing in the plaza, the music wafting softly through the night air. Tom halted his horse at the corner of the plaza. He looked across at the troops barracks, and at the sheriff's office, in which a single lamp burned. Troops thronged the plaza, some of them drunk, some sober. Two of them were fighting with their fists behind the bandstand, and a small crowd had gathered to watch.

Tom said: "Wait here. Keep your eyes open." And he headed across toward the sheriff's office.

He burst in anxiously. "Durand, Hazel hasn't come back from town. You seen her?"

Durand sat comfortably with his feet up on the desk. His swivel chair creaked as he took them down. He grinned at Tom. "She's with De Chelly. Been with him all afternoon."

"Where are they now?"

"Simmer down, Tom. Take it easy. You're not going to help anybody barging around looking for trouble. De Chelly didn't force her to go with him. She went of her own free will. I'd suggest that you go home, before you end up in De Chelly's prison."

Tom scowled. "Damn you, I'm not worried about De Chelly. But someone else followed her all the way from McGuire's. I think it was Ziegler."

The sheriff shrugged in a way that intimated he thought Tom was unduly alarmed. "Schofield ain't the kind to fight women, Tom. Now relax and go on home."

Tom grunted: "To hell with you." He went outside. Behind him he could hear the sheriff muttering, but could not distinguish his words.

He stopped a trooper who was staggering along the gallery. "Where'll I find your major, Yank? Which is the door to his quarters?"

The trooper pointed drunkenly. "It'sh right there, Johnny. But what the hell you wantin' with that son-of-a . . . ?"

Tom didn't wait for him to finish. He was running along the gallery, running desperately, afraid of what he might find.

Ziegler entered the rear door to De Chelly's quarters. He saw the major struggling with Hazel. Then he saw the girl break away and dart toward the door. Suddenly Ziegler realized the possibilities of this situation.

His boss, Schofield, hated and feared De Chelly, for De Chelly knew that Schofield's claim to Matt Cady's place was built on fraud. Only recently De Chelly had demanded, and gotten, a larger cut of the proceeds. And Ziegler knew that Schofield intended eventually to kill De Chelly. Here was a golden opportunity, not only to kill De Chelly, but to shift the blame for it onto Tom Cady and Doc McGuire.

What would be simpler than to kill De Chelly, then pursue Hazel, bring her back and kill her, too? Who could connect Schofield or Ziegler with the crimes? Durand would reason that De Chelly had lured Hazel to his quarters and attacked her. So would the military. The man's reputation was well established among the bluebellies. They would reason further that Hazel had fought him and that he killed her, accidentally perhaps, in his drunken fury at being balked. They would also believe that Cady had come upon the scene and killed De Chelly for revenge. Even if Cady were nowhere near town, his protests of innocence would do him no good. He would be convicted even though he had a dozen witnesses to testify for him.

Ziegler began to grin widely, and his grin faded only slightly as Hazel broke away, burst through the door and out onto the gallery. He simply noted the direction she took. After that he moved with all the swiftness and precision of a striking diamondback. De Chelly was still on his hands and knees, struggling to get up, when Ziegler's knife sank into his back. Scarcely breaking stride, Ziegler crossed the room and bolted through the outside door.

Behind him he could hear De Chelly choking on his own blood, and then a long sigh, and after that the thud and clatter of De Chelly's body collapsing upon the floor. Looking down the street, he saw Hazel just turning the corner away from the plaza. Ziegler ran tirelessly and silently, as the hunting wolf runs once he sights his prey.

Tom saw Hazel dash from the door to De Chelly's quarters. She did not pause on the gallery, but instead fled along it as though pursued by the devil. Relief ran through Tom so strongly that it weakened his arms and legs. Then he saw Ziegler burst through the door, glance down the street, turn, and run after Hazel.

What Ziegler planned, Tom had no way of knowing. He only knew the need to get Ziegler's scrawny neck between his hands. Tom yelled at Tonio, then broke into a run himself. He sprinted for the first 100 yards, and managed to cut the distance between himself and Ziegler in half.

He entered the dark side street then, and was forced to slow down. These were the little streets, where the poor of Matadero lived. They reeked with the stench of garbage, of sewage, of dead and unremoved animal carcasses. The soft strumming of guitars came from the open windows of a few of the miserable adobe hovels. Mangy, snarling dogs yapped at Tom's heels, but he was able to keep track of Ziegler. The dogs were snapping at Ziegler's heels, too, heralding his continuing progress in this man-made jungle.

Somewhere a woman screamed, and a man cursed in Spanish. Somewhere a drunken laugh issued forth. A cat, flushed from its hiding place by the noise of the dogs, scooted between Tom's legs and tripped him. He staggered, and almost fell, then recovered and went on, beginning to grow short of wind now.

A door opened and a pan of dishwater splashed into the street at Tom's feet. He leaped the puddle and went on. The cat raced ahead of him, and the dogs that had been snapping at him suddenly lost interest and took up the pursuit of the cat. The changed tone of their baying drew the other dogs away from Ziegler, too. The whole pack veered into a narrow side street.

Tom stopped and listened. In the house beside him he could hear voices quarreling shrilly in Spanish. Absently his mind followed the wife's words, which profanely accused the husband of infidelity. But he heard no sound of Ziegler's progress, and for a moment he felt panicky and helpless.

This part of Matadero was now a cacophony of sound—dogs barking, the cat snarling and spitting from the fence where it had made its stand, quarreling voices, and the band's muted, brassy bleats from the bandstand in the plaza. But no sound came from the hunting Ziegler, or from the fleeing Hazel.

A waning, crescent moon cast its feeble glow upon the sordid scene, giving it a beauty not possible in stronger light. Tom moved on. He had to. He might take the wrong turn, but, if he didn't risk it, he would be left too far behind for help. And then he began to realize how much Hazel had come to mean to him. Cold she might seem, and defensive. But he knew this was just a surface shell of protection. Underneath, she was all a man could ask. Her wild response to his kiss had told him that. If Ziegler touched her. . . . Blindly Tom moved on, a killer tonight if he never had been one before.

Back in the plaza, Tonio Polidoro watched Tom run into the side street. Something had happened over there in the commandant's quarters. Something had happened, and Tonio, ever alert for a way to hurt Tom, proposed to find out what it was. He moved casually toward the open door, glancing up and down the gallery at the few people who were strolling there. There was the drunken soldier who Tom had questioned. He was supporting himself stupidly from one of the columns, staring blearily out at the band in the lighted square. There was a group of boisterous troopers who had just come from a *cantina* down the street. There was an oldster, staring intently at the fight out behind the bandstand. Probably they had not even seen Hazel run from the major's quarters. Probably they had seen neither Ziegler nor Tom. Or if they had, they had paid no heed.

Tonio walked quietly and unobtrusively along the gallery until he came to De Chelly's quarters. Then, with a furtive look up and down the street, he slipped inside and closed the door. For a moment he stood quite still, listening. Then he fumbled in his pocket for a match and struck it.

De Chelly lay sprawled on the floor in a pool of blood. A knife protruded from his back. Tonio knelt briefly by his side. The match burned his fingers and he dropped it. Carefully he reached out and touched De Chelly's outflung arm. He located the wrist and felt it for pulse. There was none.

Tonio's throat went dry. Suppose someone found him here? What chance would there be to convince them that he hadn't committed the murder?

He got up and tiptoed to the door. He opened it slightly and peered outside. Seeing no one, he slipped through quickly and closed it behind him. Breathing heavily, he looked up and down the gallery. The old man still sat on the walk, watching the fight out behind the bandstand. Five or six soldiers were coming down the walk, heading for their quarters. Tonio slipped back inside and waited until they passed. Then, having made up his mind, he stepped out onto the gallery and headed directly for Durand's office.

He smiled to himself. His whole body tingled as if the wine of triumph flowed in his veins. He had intended to kill Cady, but this was better. This was infinitely better.

Durand had reinstalled his feet on the desk top. He did not remove them when Tonio came in. He just took Tonio in, from the ragged duck brush jacket to the worn straw sandals and dirty protruding toes, and he yawned.

Tonio said hesitantly, hat held nervously in both hands: "*Señor,* I come to report a crime."

Durand's feet hit the floor.

Tonio went on, growing more nervous: "I have seen the *Señorita* McGuire run from the house of *el commandante.* I have seen the *Señor* Cady run in. Then he came out and I fear he has done harm to the Yankee major. You must come and see, *Señor* Sheriff. You must come see at once. Perhaps the major needs our help."

Durand cursed softly. But he moved as he cursed.

XIII

Tom prowled the narrow back streets of the town like a hunting cat. He strained to catch any small, telltale sound that would betray Ziegler's location or Hazel's. A dozen times he hesitated at the yawning mouth of a narrow alley or side street. A dozen times he made a choice, based upon his judgment of which turn a frightened, fleeing girl might take. At last, he heard it—Hazel's terrified, lost scream. The scream ended abruptly, as if a hand had been clamped roughly over her mouth.

Tom Cady began to run, careless of noise now, interested only in speed. A door opened and a man called querulously—"*¿Qué es?*"—as Tom came pounding into sight. The door slammed and he heard a bar clatter into place.

He swung around a corner, colliding with a man on mule back. The mule kicked out, and one of his hoofs struck Tom's shoulder and sent him rolling.

He cursed and struggled to his feet. His left shoulder and arm were numb. Down the alleyway he went, running, wondering if he had passed the pair in the darkness. Then he heard it—scuffling feet, panting, the rustle and thump of a wild struggle. He saw them. He saw Ziegler's gun rise and fall, and Hazel's body go limp. He yelled raggedly: "Ziegler! God damn you, turn . . . !"

Ziegler whirled, dropping the girl to the ground. Flame spat from his fisted gun.

In the faint light of the waning crescent moon, he made a deadly, crouched shape there against the adobe wall. Hazel lay at his feet, pitifully crumpled and still. Tom Cady forgot that he carried a gun. He forgot everything save his overwhelming need to get the skinny, deadly Ziegler between his hands.

He rushed, and again Ziegler's gun spat. But the light was bad and Ziegler was growing panicky. Already too much time had passed. He had to get back to the plaza, fast, with the body of the unconscious girl. He had to return her to De Chelly's quarters before someone discovered the major's body.

He fired a third shot, and this time Tom stumbled. The lead slug had hit like a club but it didn't slow him down for more than a stride. He struck Ziegler with his shoulder and drove the man back against the wall with a force that expelled Ziegler's breath in an explosive grunt.

Ziegler brought up a knee, and pain worse by far than bullet shock spread upward in a sickening wave from Tom Cady's groin. He struck out blindly, and caught Ziegler's pointed chin with the heel of his right hand. Ziegler's head snapped back, striking the wall behind him with a dull, sodden *thud*. He sagged, then, sliding down the wall.

Tom reached down and gathered a handful of his shirt front. He yanked Ziegler up, and battered him back against the wall. Half unconscious, Ziegler brought his gun around in a purely convulsive gesture. It slammed against the side of Cady's head.

For an instant Tom stood there, stunned. Ziegler broke free from his clutching hands, and crawled on hands and knees out in the middle of the alley. There he sat, resting elbows on knees, sighting carefully along his gun barrel.

Tom slumped, shaking his head, trying desperately to clear it. The gun in Ziegler's two hands jumped and bucked. Flame laced out again from its muzzle.

Tom felt a blow in his thigh exactly like the one delivered to his shoulder by the mule's hoof. And then the leg would no longer support his weight. It was almost like watching someone else fall, so unreal did it seem. The world tipped, and fell onto its side. Tom felt the ground against shoulder and hip.

He struggled to sit up. Ziegler was a crouched, hazily unreal shape out there in the middle of the alley. Tom's hand, pressing against the ground, encountered something hard and cold and smooth. His gun. His hand closed weakly over its grips. He tugged at it, but had not the strength to pull it clear.

Ziegler got up and approached, his gun glinting oddly in the dim moonlight. To Tom's eyes, he seemed to be three men instead of one. Tom had the wry and errant thought: *Which one should I shoot at? The one on the left? The right? Or the one in the middle?* He knew Ziegler would kill him now, if he could, with a shot fired from a range of no more than a few inches. Then he'd take Hazel. . . .

Tom tugged savagely at his gun again, rolling a little to take his body weight from its holster. Suddenly it pulled clear. *Wait*, his mind told him. *Wait until you can jam the muzzle against him. Wait until there's only one of him to shoot at.* But he couldn't wait. He fired with the gun steadied on

121

his unwounded thigh, pointing it as he might have pointed a finger at the approaching, solidifying middle shape.

This time he scored a hit, although not in the vital spot at which he aimed. Ziegler's gun clattered to the ground. He clutched his right shoulder with his left hand. Even in the poor light, Tom could see the dark red shine of blood oozing out between his fingers.

Tom fired again, missing cleanly. Ziegler stooped and recovered his gun with his left hand. Tom shot again, missing this time, too.

Ziegler threw him a glance, then turned, and ran, weaving back and forth from alley wall to alley wall, colliding violently with it each time he did. Even after he was out of sight, Tom could hear him, plowing through discarded tin cans, bowling over heaps of trash, and cursing bitterly and loudly, although almost incoherently.

Tom shoved his gun back into its holster, fighting the nausea that rolled in him, the weakness caused by his loss of blood. He fumbled at the buttons of his shirt, then exasperatedly tore the shirt from his back. Without attempting to arrange it in strips, he wound it around his leg to staunch the flow of blood.

Hazel was stirring, moaning faintly. Cady crawled to her, dragging the numb and useless leg behind.

She came awake, and she fought him until he said harshly: "Cut it out! Ziegler's gone. This is Tom."

It seemed to bring back her senses. She said: "You're hurt!"

"Yeah. I don't know how bad. We'd better get to some light and see."

"Can you walk?"

"I can try, if you'll help me up. How bad are you hurt?"

She laughed nervously. "I've got a headache, the

granddaddy of all headaches."

He was scared, plain scared as she helped him to his feet. His leg bone might be shattered. Deliberately, stubbornly he put his full weight on the injured leg. The pain was terrible, but it supported him without crumpling. He breathed a long, slow sigh of relief. A shattered bone would never have done that.

The effort had soaked him with sweat. Wind, blowing against his damp body, chilled him and he began to shiver. Hazel murmured: "Try now, Tom. I'll hold up the bad side, so don't be afraid to put your weight on me."

He took a step, then another, putting his full weight on Hazel instead of on his injured leg. Her strength held him up without faltering. He had the transient thought that Annemarie Bassett would have been useless in this situation. She would have left him alone, and run screaming toward the plaza.

He could feel the warmth of blood below the wound clear down to his foot. Again that feeling of urgency possessed him. If the bullet had severed an artery. . . . He said: "Stop at the first house. Let's get some light on this thing."

"You need a doctor."

"Sure. I need a hole in my head, too. There's something all wrong with this. Why didn't De Chelly come after you? He didn't strike me as the kind of man that would let a woman get away without at least trying to run her down. So he's knocked cold or dead. Either way, it'll be damned unsafe for us around the plaza tonight. Find a house."

"All right, Tom." Her tone was subdued. He knew she blamed herself for bringing this situation about, but he was sure she had not. Probably she had been afraid to refuse De Chelly. Certainly she had not encouraged him.

They had gone no more than a laborious 100 yards when

Hazel propped him against a wall and knocked upon a door. Again that timid question—"*¿Qué es?*"—and Hazel launched into a hasty explanation in Spanish. The door opened a little wider. Hazel helped Tom inside.

Thereafter, she wasted no time at all. With Tom's knife she slit his trouser leg and peeled it back to reveal the ugly wound from which blood flowed steadily. The bullet had gone through cleanly, missing both bones and arteries. Another bullet, the one that had made Tom stumble, had grazed the flesh six inches above the second wound.

In rapid Spanish, Hazel asked for a bottle of tequila, and poured it, straight, over the wound. Tom held to his fainting senses with grim determination, but turned a ghastly shade of gray.

Then, with cloths she could only hope were clean, Hazel tied up the worst of the two wounds, afterward soaking the bandage with the remains of the tequila. Tom gave a silver dollar, his last, to the Mexican woman and her aging husband. Then he and Hazel slipped out again into the night.

He spoke between clenched teeth. "We've got to have horses. We've got to get into the brush. If we stay in town, we're done."

He stood there, trying to remember the town, to recall where the stables and liveries were, and in the midst of the effort he noticed the absence of band music from the plaza. Instead, he heard the low murmur from many throats, not a menacing murmur but a jubilant one.

A boy came racing along the back streets, crying something excitedly in Spanish, and suddenly Tom understood the words. "De Chelly is dead! De Chelly is dead!"

Hazel gave a gasp of horror. Tom's stomach felt empty and cold. For soon along the streets of Matadero would thunder the hoofs of Yankee cavalrymen. Houses would be searched, the poor and the furtive run down and manhandled. The vengeance of the cavalry would seek the guilty but would punish many of the innocent in haste and in anger.

"I didn't kill him," Hazel whispered frantically.

Tom laughed bitterly. "Of course you didn't. Ziegler did. The thing is, Durand knows I went to De Chelly's quarters looking for you. He doesn't know Ziegler was there at all. So I'm the man they want, and, if we don't get the hell out of here, I'm the man they'll get."

Helped by Hazel, he moved along, forced to zigzag because of the twisting, narrow streets, but keeping to a westerly direction away from the plaza and toward the river. He considered trying to escape by boat on the river, but gave it up. No. He wanted a horse. He wanted to lose himself in the brush country. Only in the brush would he have a chance.

The 100 or so men in De Chelly's cavalry troop could not comb out the brush country. Indeed, 100 men could become lost in it. Tom's only chance lay in reaching it, in gaining its thorny, tangled safety.

A dozen times in the next hour they cowered in doorways or in the narrow passageways between buildings as a patrol of cavalry thundered past. A brisk wind came up, bringing Tom the faint smell of manure. He followed the wind, knowing that eventually it would lead him to the corral.

At last they reached it, hearing behind them the thundering hoofs of still another cavalry patrol. Tom and Hazel entered the gate in the adobe corral wall, fully aware that the enclosure might become a trap. Tom did not expect the corral attendant to be awake, and he began looking around for a rope.

A soft voice startled him coming out of the pale darkness. "*Aquí, amigo*. If you are pursued by the *yanquis,* come this way quickly. They are too near to give you time to catch and saddle horses. But I have two saddled here by the other gate."

The Mexican hostler appeared to lead the way. Tom hobbled after him, still supported on the one side by Hazel. They reached the two horses just as the patrol burst through the main gate. At first the patrol milled wildly, and then a harsh voice bellowed: "You, in there! Come here!"

The Mexican murmured almost soundlessly—"*Vaya con Dios, amigos.*"—then raised his voice to the officer: "*Sí, señor.* I come."

Tom pulled himself into the saddle by the strength of his arms. Hazel mounted the other horse quickly and lightly and led the way at a quiet walk through the narrow gate in the wall.

As they cleared the gate, Tom heard the officer's voice again: "You missin' any hosses, Mex? You seen any strangers tonight?"

"*No, Señor Teniente.*"

Tom headed back into the jungle of shacks and threaded his silent way along the little streets until he came out on the northern end of town. Here, he crossed an open clearing half a mile wide and disappeared into the thicket with Hazel riding closely at his heels. In darkness, progress was painfully slow, but by the time dawn streaked the eastern sky with gray, five miles of thicket lay between them and the town of Matadero.

At dawn, weakness flowed over Tom like a tide and he toppled from his horse. Barely conscious, he heard Hazel's quick movements as she led the horses away into the brush and tied them.

She returned immediately and knelt at his feet. He saw her through a haze of pain, her hair a tangled mass, her face scratched and bleeding. Her dress hung in tatters, and torn wisps of petticoat dangled beneath its hem. With infinite care she removed the bandage from his wound. But in spite of her care, pain spread from the wound as an oil stain spreads upon the water. Blackness descended like a curtain over his vision and he fainted.

XIV

The day came and went while Tom lay unconscious, and it fell full dark again before he opened his eyes. His first awareness was of the brush sounds around him, his second of Hazel sitting so close beside him, bathing his face with a damp cloth. A small fire burned half a dozen yards away.

Fever had ravaged his body, leaving it weak and trembling. Pain lived imprisoned in his leg, like a live bed of coals in a stove. Now, however, most of the fever was gone and his mind was clear. He remembered all that had happened last night in Matadero, and carefully he eased himself up to an elbow. Exertion and pain made cold sweat break out on his forehead. He grinned ruefully. "How's the leg looking by now?"

Hazel looked drawn and tired, but her eyes were soft. "I think it will be all right, Tom. It's red and raw, but I think our tequila did the trick."

"We can't stay here. We need food . . . and water."

"We've got to stay here. There's no place else to go. They'll be searching for you all through the thicket."

"Where are we?"

"About five miles from town. You can't travel, Tom,

and, besides, they'll be watching every shack in the thicket."

He nodded at the damp cloth in her hand. "You've found water?"

"Yes. A seep. I dug down about a foot and a half with a stick. It will do, Tom. It will be enough for a while."

"How about food?"

She smiled. "I risked a shot with your gun. We have fresh wild pork hanging over there in that mesquite tree."

He regarded her with new respect. "I was going to give you hell for getting involved with De Chelly, but how can I now?"

"Go ahead, Tom. I guess I deserve it."

"How'd it happen?"

She flushed. "It wouldn't have happened if I'd had a little more faith. I thought you'd killed Stutz, and I was afraid to make the major mad for fear he'd throw you and Dad in that dungeon of his."

Cady said: "I did kill Stutz . . . in a way. He picked a fight with me that night and pulled a knife. Fell on his own knife. Doc and I buried him out in the brush."

Hazel was silent for a long time. At last she said: "What are we going to do? The cavalry is after you for killing De Chelly and you haven't a chance in the world of proving you didn't do it. We can't go back home. Where can we go?"

"I'll think of something, Hazel. They want me to run. They want me clear out of the country. But why? That's what I want to know."

Hazel opened her mouth, then closed it again.

"What were you going to say?" Tom prompted.

"Nothing."

He lay still for a while. Hazel got up and arranged some

meat on sticks over the fire.

"Damn it," Tom said. "Tonio should have set Durand straight. He saw you run out of De Chelly's place with Ziegler after you. He knows I never even went inside."

Hazel turned. "That's what I was going to mention a minute ago. About Tonio. I talked to Sheriff Durand yesterday. I asked him some questions about your father and the men he killed. Somehow or other I can't help but think there's a connection between your father and the things that are happening now."

"What'd you find out? Something about Tonio?"

"Only that there was a fellow named Polidoro among the men your father killed. Ambrosio Polidoro. I think he may have been related to Tonio. Polidoro certainly isn't a common name."

"What if he is related?"

"Tom, haven't you noticed the way Tonio looks at you . . . almost as though he hated you?"

Tom had noticed, often enough, and Miguel had mentioned it. If Tonio were related to this Ambrosio Polidoro, he might have taken the job with Doc in the hopes of. . . . Tom shook his head. Why would a man seek revenge against the son of the man he hated? Still, stranger things had happened. And if Tonio was not seeking revenge, why hadn't he told Sheriff Durand that Tom could not possibly have killed De Chelly?

"What else did you find out?" he asked.

"That all the men your father killed were working for Schofield."

Tom gaped at her in amazement. "You're sure?"

She nodded. "Durand acted strangely when I asked him about Matt. He didn't seem to want to talk, but I kept after him. Finally he managed to remember the names of the men Matt killed. And later he let it slip that they were working for Schofield."

For a few minutes Tom lay still, staring at the stars. More than ever now he was convinced that Schofield knew something about his father's death. He had wondered, when he first arrived, at Schofield's apparently senseless animosity. He had wondered why both Durand and Schofield had been so anxious that he leave the country. Had they feared that he might discover the truth about Matt's death?

He frowned in puzzlement. What was the truth about Matt's death? Matt had gone hog-wild. There had been dozens of eyewitnesses to it. Perhaps, then, Schofield's and Durand's complicity in his death lay in the things that had led up to it. Schofield and Durand must be involved in the reasons behind it.

Tom felt suddenly impatient with his helplessness. He wanted to get to town, to force the truth out of Tonio. He wanted to get his hands on Schofield's throat and make him talk. Matt had not gone berserk at all, the way he saw it now. He had been attacked, under the guise of a drunken fight, and had died defending himself.

Hazel brought him a chunk of broiled pork. Since she had no vessel in which to carry water, she brought him a soaked cloth, and with this he eased his throat.

Then she lay down beside him while the fire slowly died. She was dirty, mussed, and tired. And beautiful, Tom thought—more so than ever before. Today her guard was down and there was a helpless, earthy quality about her that he had never noticed before. Tonight she was beat, and scared, and dependent upon him in spite of his helplessness.

He watched her sleep while impatience raged in him. He could feel his leg swelling and stiffening, and he knew many days must pass before he could ride. He felt a stir of tenderness for her—and hopelessness, for he could see nothing but death ahead for himself.

In the minds of the military, he had already been tried and convicted. He was the son of Matt Cady, who had gone berserk in the plaza three years ago. And now he had fulfilled everyone's expectations by killing De Chelly. Even if he wanted to, he'd get no chance to surrender. The soldiers would shoot him down like a mad dog. Schofield would use the convenient fact of De Chelly's death as an excuse to join the hunt, and Schofield was infinitely more dangerous than all the Union troops.

What, then, could he do? Right now, wait. That was all. When his wound healed a little, when he felt stronger, he could try getting to the bottom of all this. By seeing Tonio, and Schofield, and Durand.

The night passed, but Tom did not sleep. At dawn, Hazel opened her eyes, oddly child-like and defenseless upon first awakening. Her tongue came out and wet her lips and she swallowed with difficulty. Her small voice revealed shame.

"I slept, and let you watch."

"Why not? You watched all day yesterday while I slept." He tried to get up, failed, and fell back. His leg had puffed, stiffened. Weak or not, he had to exercise it to keep the stiffness down.

He looked around, spied a suitable mesquite branch, and sent Hazel to fetch it. Thereafter, he busied himself whittling out a crutch while Hazel built up the fire and cooked more chunks of meat. There was some chance that the smoke would be seen, but they had to take it. Without food, they would die. And pork could not be eaten raw.

After they had eaten, Hazel brought him a cloth soaked

with water. He recognized it as part of her petticoat. Then she went to the horses and led them, one by one, to the seep she had dug out. They drank noisily. After they finished, she picketed them out in a different spot so they could graze.

The day passed with agonizing slowness. Tom kept busy whittling at his crutch. Near noon, Tom finished it and laboriously walked about twenty yards and back. The effort exhausted him. His leg throbbed with pain waves that dizzied him. He collapsed to the ground, aware that the leg was bleeding again, and glad, because the bleeding would carry off infection.

He slept throughout the afternoon, and walked again in early evening, this time gritting his teeth and making a circle nearly forty yards in diameter. Hazel's petticoat had been used almost entirely for bandages, and tonight, as she put the last of it upon his wound, she said steadily: "Tom, I've got to go home after bandages and whiskey and food. Besides, we've got to know what's going on."

Fear for her made his voice unnecessarily harsh. "I can tell you what's going on. They're watching Doc's place, just waiting for one of us to turn up. They know you're with me . . . at least Schofield does . . . and they know you've been helping me. Wait a day or two. Then get clear out of the country. It's the only way you'll ever be safe."

It was the first time either of them had admitted that the outlook was hopeless. Hazel knelt at Tom's feet. She had less security right now than ever before in all her life, yet she seemed less afraid. There was a steadiness about her, a calmness that touched Tom to the quick.

He reached out and caught her hands, dirty hands, scarred by brush. He said soberly: "Hazel, I'm all right now. I'll be able to travel in a day or two. I want you to take one of the horses and go to Austin. Don't come back until this thing has quieted down."

"No," she said.

"Do you know what they'll do to you if they catch you?"

"What will they do, Tom? What can they do? I've committed no crime and neither have you."

He laughed bitterly. "Do you think they care about a thing like that? Hell, these are occupation troops. Their commandant has just been killed. I've been named the killer, and, if they don't catch me, there's no safety in Texas for any Union trooper. They know it and the people know it. Do you think they'd let me go even if they found that I didn't kill De Chelly? Hell, no. They couldn't, Hazel. Maybe you think they're only after me and that they won't bother you because you're a woman. Don't fool yourself. They know you've been with me and they know you were with De Chelly the night he was killed. They'd rather hang you than me, because it would scare the people worse than it would to see a man hanged."

He had hoped to frighten her into leaving him. Now he saw that he had only frightened her. Her face was bloodless, but he saw courage and determination in her eyes that nothing could ever frighten away.

"How the hell do you expect to get near the house without getting caught?" he said.

"I won't be seen," she said.

She shaped her mouth precisely and made a series of sharp noises so much like coyote yaps that Tom looked around in spite of himself. She gave the hoot of an owl, and after that the peculiar chirping of a cricket. Then she smiled at Tom. "Dad taught me those things when I was a little girl. I can draw him away from the house and nobody will be the wiser. He'll get me what I want and tell me the news."

She got up and built a small fire. She broiled some more chunks of wild pork.

Tom ate ravenously. The fire died, and Hazel scattered the embers to kill them. She lay down across from him and stared at the sky, waiting for darkness.

He had no fear that she would lose her way, for Hazel possessed the same odd directional sense that all brush people have, but he did fear the slyness of Durand and Schofield, the numbers and persistence of the Yankee troops. He also knew that she had no choice. Without whiskey for disinfectant and clean bandages, his wound would not heal, indeed, would probably become gangrenous. Without food they would weaken, and they couldn't live on wild pork forever. Besides that, they needed blankets as protection against storms that might come up unexpectedly this time of year.

Darkness came and he watched her go with uneasiness and doubt. After she left, he wondered what he could do, even when he was able to travel. Where could he go? What chance did he have? He cursed. What chance? None. But he'd make a chance. He'd find out what was behind Schofield's hatred, and Durand's fear, and Tonio's betrayal. He'd find out what had touched off Matt's fury in the plaza. When he knew that, he'd have all the answers he wanted, and someone would pay.

For a while he lay still, scowling at the moonlit sky, going back over all that had happened since his return. Matt's death was beginning to tie in closer and closer with both Durand and with Schofield. Quite possibly it tied in, as well, with De Chelly's murder, for it was obvious that Schofield's man Ziegler had done the killing, probably on Schofield's orders. Was it not possible that in some way Matt had stood between Schofield and his avowed ambition to be King of Texas? Had Schofield ordered Matt killed?

Tom Cady thought so. Following this reasoning further, he decided that in some way Durand and later De Chelly had discovered Schofield's guilt. Instead of bringing him to justice, they might be blackmailing him with their silence. Sure. They probably were. But thinking it and proving it were separated by a wide gulf.

He dozed a little as the night wore on, plagued by the incessant pain in his leg. Beside him the dying coals of the fire, which Hazel had not fully extinguished, smoldered and sent up thin plumes of smoke.

It must have been this smoke that drew the cavalry patrol to the spot. Tom never knew. But long before midnight he became aware of a strangely powerful aura of uneasiness. He sat upright, at first connecting his uneasiness with fear for Hazel. Then he heard the soft nicker of his horse, picketed out fifty yards away.

He scrambled to his feet, digging hard with the homemade crutch. He stood still, listening. For a minute or so, he heard nothing. Then, downwind, he heard the answering soft nicker of another horse, muffled, as though by a hand clamped over its nostrils.

He didn't hesitate. Moving as silently and as swiftly as he could with the crutch, cursing the moon and gritting his teeth against pain, he hobbled toward his horse. Had they caught Hazel and forced her to lead them to him? No. Nothing would have made her do it. Had they followed her back, then? He doubted it. She had not been gone long enough to reach McGuire's and return. No. They must have just stumbled on him, attracted by the smell of the smoldering fire. There was not much hope in Tom. Probably he was already surrounded. But he'd been in spots like this before, during the war, and he knew that no hand is ever lost until all the cards have been played.

Still ten yards short of his horse, he heard a branch crack on the other side of the camp. He heard a low, muffled curse. He reached the horse, and the animal danced away from him nervously. Tom Cady cursed savagely under his breath. Already uneasy from the night sounds and smells, the horse was further frightened by his halting, clumsy gait. But if he didn't get to riding immediately, he'd have no chance at all.

His foot caught on the picket rope. He stooped and grabbed it up. Pulling it hand over hand, he drew the horse toward him. No time for saddle, or even for bridle. He severed the rope with a quick slash of his knife, then fashioned a quick hackamore with it. Hard to mount a bareback horse with a bad leg. Damned near impossible, regardless of how experienced a horseman you were.

A shout lifted as a cavalryman reached his camp and found him gone. There was a loud crashing in the brush as they closed in.

Tom drove his homemade crutch against the ground. Using it like a vaulting pole, he flung himself upward by the sheer strength of his arms. If the horse danced away now. . . .

He felt his forward leg slide across the horse's back. His wounded leg struck the horse's near side with force enough to wrench a strangled cry from his throat. But he was astride, and the horse was leaping away.

Blinded, dizzied by pain, Tom Cady charged directly into the troopers' midst. A carbine barked, and another, and then a commanding voice shouted: "Hold your fire, you god-damn' fools! You want to kill each other?" The voice was still the barest instant, then lifted again: "Horse holders! Horse holders!"

But Cady was through their line. Through in the brush. In spite of pain, he chuckled softly to himself. Not a man of that patrol could touch his brush popper's speed in the thicket. Not a man could pursue him more than half a mile.

He reined in his wildly running horse, even though he heard them coming behind him, making all the noise of a cyclone tearing through the mesquite. He was away. He was free. But if he knew the cavalry, they'd post a guard back there against the possibility of his return. Unless he could intercept Hazel, she'd walk right into their arms.

XV

Gradually the sounds of the pursuing patrol faded behind Tom Cady, but he continued to ride recklessly. He could never hope to intercept Hazel as she returned. His only hope lay in reaching McGuire's before she began her return.

Actually it was easier for him, riding bareback, than it would have been with a saddle. Even so, his leg flopped back and forth with the movement of the horse and the wound began to bleed freely. Blood soaked through the bandage and trickled into his boot. His weakness increased as he rode, until his head felt light, until his body became weak and clammy with cold sweat. But still he rode and the miles flowed behind, and gradually the pain became less and the sweat dried on his skin.

He couldn't quit, and he couldn't get sicker. He had to go on, and he had to grow stronger. And somehow his body adjusted itself to the demands of the stark necessity in his mind, and began to heal itself as he rode, on and on and on.

By ghostly moonlight, he saw the old house towering

above the brush while he was yet a quarter mile away. He slowed and began his circle.

He yipped like a coyote, then hooted like an owl. Lastly he made the chirping sound of a cricket, although not as skillfully as Hazel had. He stopped to listen, holding his breath with anxiety. A minute passed. Another. Finally he heard the answering cry of a coyote, but no more. The place must be guarded, then, or Hazel would have followed her coyote cry with that of the owl and the cricket.

Tom Cady headed toward the sound cautiously. He dared not dismount, without his crutch. So great was his relief when he saw her that he slid from his horse, the wounded leg forgotten. He stepped toward her and his leg gave way. He fell.

With a small cry of dismay, she came to him and knelt by his side. And suddenly she was in his arms, her face wet with her tears. "Tom, what are you doing here? You shouldn't be riding. Your leg. . . ."

"Damn my leg."

"Tom, what hap . . . ?"

He kissed her. He drew back and looked at her, then tightened his arms and kissed her again. This time blood seemed to roar and pound in his head. He drew back again, and grinned.

"You're a lot of woman, Hazel. A hell of a lot of woman."

"Tom, you're teasing."

"Teasing, hell. If it wasn't for this leg. . . ."

"Tom! There are troopers within a hundred yards of you. Are you crazy?"

"Crazy about you."

Her arms went tightly about his neck and she buried her face in his chest. "Tom, what are we going to do?"

138

"Get married. Raise kids."

She began to cry softly. "What chance have we got for that? Every trooper in Texas is looking for you. Durand, too. And Schofield."

He sobered. "What did you find out here? Have you seen Doc?"

She nodded. "He's getting some things together for me now."

"What news did he have?"

"Only what we already know. They're looking for you, dead or alive. They've posted a thousand dollars' reward."

"What else? Has Schofield bothered Doc?"

She shook her head. "Ivy and Doc are guarding the house, though there's not much danger here with all the troopers around. Miguel is camping out in the brush with two new men gathering cattle."

"What about Tonio?"

"Durand's holding him in jail as a material witness."

"Then I've got to go to town." Tom stirred. "Help me up."

"Not until you've eaten and I've bandaged that leg again." She gave a little grimace of frustration and concern. "Tom, don't go at all. Please. Wait until you're well."

"If I do, I'll finish getting well in jail, Hazel. I've got to go tonight."

Hazel whirled at a sound behind her. Tom saw Doc easing almost silently through the brush. Doc didn't speak. He just began loading the things he carried on Hazel's horse.

Then he came over and watched Hazel re-bandage Tom's leg. After that he helped Tom mount. All this while he kept looking uneasily over his shoulder, as though expecting a troop of cavalry to burst from the brush.

Hazel mounted her heavily-laden horse. Doc peered at Tom's shadowed face. "Where'll you be? How can I reach you? What do you want me to do?"

Tom smiled wearily at him. "Just what you're doing, Doc. Watch the house. Keep Miguel and his new men working if you can. Other than that, just wait. We'll make a new camp out in the brush somewhere. The less you know about where it is the better."

Doc nodded, and they rode away, walking their horses carefully until they were beyond hearing range of the house. Then they began to hurry. Dawn was not too far away.

Tom located camp about halfway between McGuire's and town, this time near a small stream that flowed toward the river. He did not dismount.

"Anything you want from town?" he asked Hazel.

"Just be careful, Tom. Promise?"

"Yes," he said, and turned to avoid further entreaties. He rode away quickly. He wanted to look back and wave, but didn't trust himself.

Be careful, she had said. She had known what he was riding into—a town where every inhabitant was a potential bounty-seeker, every man was a hunter. A $1,000 reward, Doc had said, and $1,000 was more than many of Matadero's inhabitants would earn in a lifetime.

How many hours remained until dawn? Tom scanned the sky and judged the moon, setting now behind the thicket to westward. He thought the eastern sky was beginning to pale, but could not be sure. Provided he could get into town, see Tonio, and get out again before daylight caught him, he couldn't have chosen a better time of day for what he had to do. Late enough because the night revelers would be off the streets, early enough because the early risers would still be in bed. Durand would be sleeping and so would most of the troopers.

He left his horse tied to one of the timbers that supported the bandstand and tore loose a short one for use as a cane. The nails that held it screeched protestingly, and Tom froze, listening. He heard nothing, so he hobbled across the square toward the sheriff's office.

A trooper stood sleepy guard before De Chelly's quarters. Other than that, Tom saw no one. The barracks guard must be inside.

Tom stepped into Durand's office warily. He found the sheriff sleeping in his chair, his unshaven chin resting on his chest. A single lamp burned low upon the desk.

Tom closed the heavy door and barred it. Then, prodded by the pain in his leg and his smoldering anger, he yanked the chair out from under the sheriff.

Durand came scrambling to his feet, clawing for his gun. Tom struck him a glancing blow on his bushy, leonine head with the barrel of his revolver. Durand went down with a grunt.

"Where's Polidoro?" Tom said.

Durand sat up. He rubbed a shaking hand across his head, then looked stupidly at the blood on its palm. He said: "You're a fool! You can't get away with this!"

"Where's Polidoro?" Tom repeated. He drew back his improvised cane as if it were a club.

"Don't do that! He's back there in a cell." Durand motioned toward the jail behind the office with a toss of his head, and winced.

"Lead the way," Tom said. "Don't try anything. I can't be hanged but once."

Durand shambled groggily toward the door that led to the cells. He unlocked the door and Tom followed him through, shoving the door closed behind him. Durand started to turn, but Tom's gun barrel was already descending. It cracked the sheriff's head with exactly calculated force and Durand slumped silently to the dirty floor.

Tonio sat up on a rumpled bunk in his cell and rubbed the sleep from his eyes. "You've come to get me out, *jefe?*" The words were hopeful, but his eyes were not. He couldn't conceal his fear.

Tom said: "No. I came to listen. I came to hear why you told them I killed De Chelly. You know Ziegler did that. You know I didn't even go into De Chelly's quarters. Why did you lie?"

"They beat me, *jefe*," Tonio whined.

"There isn't a mark on you, man."

"The marks have gone away."

"In two days?" Tom's voice became evenly savage. "Stop lying, Tonio. Open up and talk or I'm coming in that cell after you."

Tonio sat sullenly on the bunk, refusing to look at Tom. Tom stooped and got Durand's keys from the man's waist. He inserted one at random into the cell door. It was not the right one, so he tried another, and another. The fourth one opened the door. Tom stepped inside.

He advanced toward Tonio, hobbling but ready. "Why?" he said.

Suddenly Tonio sat bolt upright. He screeched: "Because I hate you, *cochino!* Because your father killed my brother! Because he slashed me here!" He ripped open his shirt to reveal a white, hairless scar that ran diagonally across his chest.

Tom stared at Tonio. The man was corroded with venom. Tom wondered why he had not seen it before. Hate had left Polidero's mouth permanently twisted, embittered. His eyes glared murderously. This was what hate did to the man who nurtured it. Tom said: "But why me? I wasn't even in the country at the time."

"You are his. You are his son. It is enough."

Tonio's eyes had been growing wilder. Suddenly he came to his feet and rushed across the cell.

Tom thrust his shoulder against the cell wall and raised the timber he was using as a cane. It collided with Tonio's head the instant he came within range. The man crashed into Tom, knocking him down and falling across his body. Tom's gun went clattering across the floor.

But Tonio was out. Tom rolled him off disgustedly, then climbed laboriously to his feet. He recovered his gun and went out, locking the cell door behind him.

He walked past Durand, went into the front office, and locked the jail door. He crossed the room toward the barred front door. Just as he reached for the bar, someone outside began knocking.

For an instant he shrank inside himself, feeling trapped and desperate. Had someone heard the noise from the sheriff's office? Had the trooper guards come to investigate? He shrugged, finally, with a certain fatalism. He eased the bar up and off the door. Then he yanked it open. Thrusting his gun out before him, finger curled about the trigger, what he saw almost startled him into pulling it.

Annemarie Bassett stood before him in the cold gray light of dawn, a startled and lovely vision.

She gasped: "Oh, it's you! What are you doing here? I thought. . . ."

"That I was wanted for murder? I am. Hurry up. What do you want?"

"My father wants to see the sheriff."

"He can't now. Go on home and keep quiet about seeing me."

Reserve touched her manner. "I don't believe I understand."

"Damn it, you don't have to understand." From a corner of his eyes, he caught a flash of approaching blue, dark like a trooper's coat. And then a Yankee trooper was standing there before the door, looking in.

Tom almost fired, but didn't. A shot would bring fifty troopers on the run. They would be blowing "Reveille" anyhow, in a few minutes. Soon the gallery would be crowded with soldiers.

So he did the only thing he could. His arm went around the girl's small waist. He pulled her to him so fiercely that her breath expelled in a pained gasp. He said: "Come in, trooper. Or shall I kill her?"

The trooper's mouth fell open. He was a tall, rangy man, somewhat stooped. He said breathlessly—"I'm comin', Cady."—and stiffened. "But if you hurt that girl. . . ."

"I won't hurt her if you do as you're told."

The trooper sidled into the office.

"You alone?" Tom said.

The trooper nodded mutely.

"What do you want?" Tom asked. "What did you come for?"

"I heard a noise. I saw Miss Bassett. . . ."

"All right. All right. Get on back there in the jail."

Annemarie Bassett began to struggle. Her squirming wrenched Cady's wounded leg. He winced, and then he cuffed her on the side of the head with the heel of his hand. She gasped with outrage.

The trooper looked as though he might protest, but changed his mind and went into the jail. Before he closed the door, Tom said: "Don't give the alarm, soldier, because

I've got Miss Bassett and I'll keep her until I'm clear. You understand?"

The trooper grunted. Cady locked the door. He released the girl. She whirled and glared at him.

"Well, I never!" she said.

Tom Cady said: "Shut up. Go on ahead of me. My horse is out by the bandstand."

She swung a hand. It whacked against his cheek, sharp and loud. He grabbed her wrist. Then he had to grin. She was so mad she was trembling.

"Move," he said. "Or do I have to hold onto you?"

"Don't you touch me!" She turned and marched outside. She crossed the gallery, her back stiff with indignation. Tom hobbled behind. Looking up and down the street and across the plaza, he saw only two or three Mexicans going sleepily to work.

Over her shoulder she asked: "Why did you do it?"

"Do what?"

"Kill Major De Chelly. Was it over that little brush wench of yours?"

"You're a snob, Miss Bassett. This will come as quite a shock to you, but I didn't kill De Chelly. Tonio is lying when he says I did."

"Why should he lie?"

"Because he hates the name Cady," Tom said wearily. "My father killed his brother. Now forget it, Miss Bassett."

But she wouldn't. "I've heard about your father."

"Everybody has. And they're all more than willing to believe I killed De Chelly because of what my old man did."

They reached the spot where Tom's horse was tied. He mounted and she blinked in surprise. "You're letting me go?"

"Yes. With apologies for losing my temper. But you hurt

145

me back there with your kicking."

For a moment she seemed to be studying him. "What would you say if I told you I didn't believe you were guilty?"

"I'd say you were an empty-headed little fool. Now go on back to your father."

He started to rein away. Annemarie stamped her foot in the dust. "Mister Cady, you're a pig-headed idiot!"

"Maybe." He withheld his grin, and asked seriously: "Will you be all right going home?"

"Of course I will. Nobody in Matadero . . . with the possible exception of yourself . . . would dare harm the daughter of Silas Bassett."

"Why? Who's he?"

"You don't know?"

"Would I ask if I did?"

She drew herself up, and thereupon gave away her father's carefully guarded secret. "He's the emissary of the President, come to investigate complaints against the military authorities here."

Tom whistled. Good God! Of all the women in Texas, he had to kidnap this one! He said—"Good bye."—and, across the plaza, a bugle squalled the first notes of "Reveille". Tom whirled his horse and set his spurs. He rode at a swift gallop northward, through the waking town and toward the safety of the thicket. His trip had accomplished nothing. He hadn't learned a thing he did not already know.

He thought of Hazel, waiting for him in the thicket. He thought of Miguel, bossing the roundup out in the brush. And suddenly he'd had all he wanted of running. Schofield would wait no longer, for this situation was made to order for him. He could move against Miguel and the gathered herd without fear of reprisal from the law. Military or no military, he was damned if he would let Schofield win by default. No. He was going back to McGuire's. He was going back to work. They might come after him. They might capture him. But, by God, they weren't going to play cat and mouse with him all over the Big Thicket.

XVI

Oddly his decision to fight back seemed to strengthen Tom. The sun came up out of the thicket and beat warmly against him and he sweated. His leg pained him, but as the miles slid behind, his weakness seemed to fade.

There was color and determination in his face as he rode into the little clearing. So much so that Hazel said hopefully: "What did you find out? Something that will clear you?"

He shook his head. "I talked to Tonio, but he jumped me before I got much out of him. I had to knock him out."

"Then nothing's changed?"

"I've changed," he said. "I'm through running away. We're going back, not to the house because there are cavalry guards there. But we're going back . . . to where Miguel and his men are working. We're going to go on fighting Schofield. I'm not much good at walking, but by God I can ride, and I'm tired of being hunted."

"They'll find out where you are and come after you."

"Maybe. But maybe I'll get a crack at Schofield before they do."

For a moment she looked as though she might argue the point. Then she saw his stubbornness, and the recklessness that came of being pushed too long and too far. She began to prepare a meal.

"I can't stop you," she murmured. "But I won't budge an inch until you eat."

He slid from his horse. He ate hungrily and drank three cups of scalding coffee. Hazel re-bandaged his leg, with the caustic observation that, if he'd stay off it for a few days, it might get a chance to heal.

They loaded up and rode away, avoiding the trails and roads through the brush. At noon, they reached the corral where Miguel had been holding the growing herd. Somehow, in bright daylight here where things were familiar, the happenings of the past several days seemed far away and unreal to Tom. He dismounted, and slept, and awoke to the low protesting bellow of cattle being driven into the clearing.

Miguel saw him and flashed a smile, but did not turn aside from his task of corralling the cattle. When he finished, he rode up with his two helpers. "Ah, *compañero,* I see you are back." He gestured toward the corral with pride. "We have now two hundred and fourteen head and all but twenty-five are branded."

"Seen anything of Schofield?"

"*Sí, señor.* Last night I rode to his place and saw him come in. He is hunting you, *amigo,* he and his crew. He has offered five hundred dollars of his own to the man who brings you down." Miguel motioned the two men forward and said: "These I have hired to help me with the work. Maximiliano and Gaspar." Both were Mexican, ragged and scarred by brush. Both wore straw sandals and no guns. Miguel said apologetically: "They speak no English, *señor,* nor will they fight. But they will work until the fighting starts."

"What would you have done if Schofield had jumped you?" Tom asked.

Miguel shrugged. "Who knows, *amigo?* Perhaps I would have fought, perhaps not. It would have been ruled by the mood I was in."

"Maybe it's a good thing I came back."

"*Sí, señor.* It is a good thing." Miguel looked at him quizzically. "You and I are tough *hombres, señor,* but not so tough that we two alone can whip Schofield and his crew. We should have Ivy and Doc here with us."

Tom turned to Hazel. "Can you get them here?"

"I can, but I'm not sure I want to. Aren't you in enough trouble, Tom?"

"Too much. This won't make it any worse," he told her grimly.

"I wish you'd give it up." She made a face, and then she smiled. "No, I don't, either. All right, Tom. I'll get Pa and Ivy."

Miguel saddled her horse with exaggerated gallantry and helped her up. Hazel rode away.

Maximiliano and Gaspar had the branding fire built and the irons hot. Tom started to ride into the corral to help, but Miguel stopped him. "Don't be a fool. Favor your leg a little. We have been branding without you several days. We can do it today."

Tom watched for a few minutes, then moved away. He made a wide circle through the brush, looking for tracks. He was under no illusions about Schofield. The man had been concentrating his energies on searching for Tom, but sooner or later the idea was going to strike Schofield that he would do better trying to make Tom come to him. And what better way was there than to destroy everything Tom had been laboring to build?

He found no fresh tracks other than those made by Miguel and Maximiliano and Gaspar, so he returned to the corral. He sat his saddle, almost wishing Schofield would show up. Then, at least, the waiting and the running would be over. Schofield no longer needed to fear the stink that killing Tom would raise. Now he could collect a reward for a killing he had previously been afraid to commit.

The day wore on slowly and at last the branding was done. Miguel and the others came from the corral, unsaddled, and rubbed down their horses. Tom built a fire and made coffee, and they sat around the fire, sipping coffee while the sun sank into the brush to the west.

Ivy and Doc and Hazel rode in as the last rays of the sun stained the sky bright orange. Hazel began to prepare supper while the men lounged near the fire and watched. Such was the scene when Durand rode out of the thicket. Tom eyed him without moving, his hand near the butt of his gun. Then he looked beyond Durand, searching the thicket for signs of a posse.

Durand said: "I'm alone, if that's what you're wondering." He rode to within twenty feet of Tom and dismounted. "You're not doing yourself any good, running like this, Cady. You didn't help yourself any by using Bassett's daughter as a hostage, either. You'll get a fair trial."

Tom laughed sourly. "You don't seriously think I'm going to believe that, do you?"

"I'm going to get you," Durand said, "or the cavalry will. You'll have a better chance if you give yourself up now."

"Go back to town, Sheriff. I didn't kill De Chelly and you know it. Try going after the man that did."

"Who?"

"Ziegler. I saw him run out of De Chelly's quarters after Hazel. I followed. He's the one that shot me, but I got him, too."

"Why would Ziegler . . . ?"

"Probably because Schofield told him to," Tom snapped, and tried a shot in the dark. "Blackmailers often get murdered, don't they?"

He thought the sheriff lost a little color, but he got no chance to pursue the subject further. Without warning, a bullet *thumped* solidly into the fire, ricocheted off the coffee pot, and whined away into space. Coffee leaked out of the bullet hole, making a hissing noise as it poured into the fire, and above the hiss Tom heard the report of a rifle. He judged it to be over 200 yards away.

He moved before the echo of the report died. So did Miguel. Maximiliano and Gaspar flattened themselves against the ground, trembling. The second bullet thumped solidly into Maximiliano's inert body. The man writhed and thrashed on the ground, and then lay still, a stain spreading across the back of his shirt. Halfway to the corral, Tom turned and flung a revolver shot uselessly at the power smoke puff across the clearing. Then, as he reached his saddle, he heard Miguel open up with his rifle, a repeating Henry.

Hazel had knelt beside Maximiliano and was rolling him over. "He's dead!" Tom yelled. "Get down or get to cover!"

Hazel got up and ran toward him. Gaspar followed. A third shot took Gaspar's leg out from under him. He fell and began to crawl, dragging the useless leg behind. Miguel was out of sight. So were Doc and Ivy Peebles.

Hazel reached Tom and flung herself down beside him, trembling. Durand stood up and yelled: "Schofield, stop firing! You've killed a man!"

Tom shouted—"He'll kill you, too, if you don't get down!"—just as the distant rifle cracked again.

Durand slapped his shoulder as though stung by a bee.

He broke into a heavy, shambling run. The rifle spoke once more. The bullet kicked up dust twenty yards beyond Durand. Durand dived into the shelter of the corral and rolled up against Tom. He sat up, knuckling dust out of his eyes.

Tom said—"Then you've been blackmailing him, too!"—and seized the man by his shirt front. "God damn you, what's he paying you to hide?"

"Nothin'," Durand said. "Nothin'. He didn't recognize me or he wouldn't have shot."

Tom snorted. "You yelled at him. He recognized you, all right. Stand up and yell at him again. Tell him who you are!"

Durand yanked free of Tom's grasp. He crawled to where he could see across the clearing. Without showing himself, he yelled: "Schofield, this is Durand! Throw down your guns and come in."

His answer was a veritable fusillade of shots. He ducked back hastily. His skin was the color of ashes. Some of the bullets had gone into the corral. A couple of steers were down, thrashing helplessly on the ground. The other cattle, smelling the blood, began to bellow frantically and to paw the ground. One of them started to horn a downed animal viciously.

Fury began to build in Tom. He crawled to Durand and thrust his revolver muzzle fiercely into Durand's back. "You son-of-a-bitch, get up and do your job, or I'll kill you where you lie!"

"Tom, I. . . ."

Tom opened his mouth to curse Durand, but he never uttered the words. Behind him, he heard the slap of a saddle thrown onto a horse's back. He rolled to look. From over on the other side of the fire, from the pile of firewood behind which he lay, Miguel shouted: "¡Señorita! No! Schofield would as soon shoot you as one of us!"

Tom thrust against the ground with his hands and came to his knees. He lunged to his feet, forgetting the bad leg, and dived toward the horse Hazel was cinching up. The leg gave way, and he fell, cursing bitterly. Struggling on the ground, he saw Hazel start toward him, her eyes brimming with tears. Then, quite plainly changing her mind, she swung into the saddle.

"Hazel!" he yelled.

She brushed her eyes with a hand. "I want those kids, Tom Cady . . . and I'll never get them unless you have help."

"Damn it, wait!"

She wheeled the plunging, frightened horse around. He reared once, and the guns across the clearing opened up. Then he bolted, thundering across the clearing.

Behind Tom, Ivy and Doc began banging away with their revolvers. Miguel fired the old Henry as fast as he could work the mechanism. When Tom looked for Hazel again, she was out of sight in the brush.

In the short time they had been pinned down, the light had faded rapidly, which perhaps accounted for the fact that Hazel had not been hit. Now, in deepening dusk light, Tom knew the danger from Schofield and his crew would increase with every minute. Soon they could creep in close, unseen.

He prodded Durand again. "You're the law in this county. Now, damn you, get up and make out like you knew it."

Perhaps Durand thought he would be safe in this deepening gray dusk. He stood up, his hands empty and held away from his body. "Schofield!" he shouted. "Schofield, stop shooting! Cady's in my custody!"

Tom heard the solid *chunk* of the bullet striking Durand before he heard the report. Durand lurched back as though struck by a monstrous fist. He sat down solidly and looked around at Tom. He showed no pain, only shock and bewilderment. From a sitting position he fell over onto his side. Then he straightened convulsively until he lay on his belly.

Tom crawled out until he could reach Durand's outstretched hand. A bullet slammed into the dirt three feet from his head. He blinked against the dust and began to cough. He seized Durand's hand and gave a jerk. Durand moved toward him about six inches. Tom jerked again, wishing he could hook a foot in the corral fence so he'd have purchase enough to pull Durand in without jerking him. He couldn't, so he jerked again.

He got Durand behind the corral and rolled him over on his back. Red was sprawling across the front of Durand's shirt.

"This is it," Durand said hoarsely. "This is the one I've been dodging for thirty years."

Tom just nodded.

Durand said, more weakly now: "Time to talk I guess. I was blackmailin' Schofield all right, but honest, Tom, I never hurt nobody."

"You killed my old man."

"An honest mistake. You got to believe that, Tom. I didn't know what was goin' on. All I saw was Matt, shootin' hell out of everybody in the plaza. I had to bring him down."

Tom waited. Durand wasn't finished, but his voice had become so weak that Tom had to lean close to hear.

"It was after I killed Matt that I found out what it was all about," Durand whispered. "Schofield bought Matt's place . . . even though he didn't have the money to pay for it . . . because he needed a base of operations before he could brand a steer. He forged a bank draft and gave it to Matt for the deed. He figured by the time Matt got around to cashing it, he'd be able to cover it. Only Matt was worried about you, Tom. He'd heard your outfit got slaughtered in Georgia. He was going to take the money and try to find you."

Durand stopped, panting, wheezing laboriously. Tom shook him. "Don't stop now. For God's sake, don't stop now!"

"No. No, I've got to tell it all." Durand rested, his breathing growing weaker and more hoarse all the time. At last he said: "Schofield found out that Matt was goin' to cash the draft. He sent his crew to pick a fight with Matt an' knock him out. They was to lift the draft off him." Durand grinned weakly. "They hadn't figured your old man was such a scrapper. Matt like to took the whole damn' bunch of them. An' that's where I came in. After I'd shot Matt, I had him hauled over to my office. Like I always do, I went through his pockets to get his stuff together. Found this draft and knowed it wasn't right. So I checked with the bank. Then I went to see Schofield."

Tom's relief was so intense that he felt weak. Matt hadn't been crazy, after all, nor had he been a killer. He'd only done a damned good job of defending himself.

"How did De Chelly come in, Sheriff?"

Durand coughed, and blood trickled from the corners of his mouth. Wheezing, he said: "I got scared of Schofield after he commenced to get big. I figured he'd try to kill me. So when the bluebelly troops came in after the war, I took De Chelly into the thing with me. I figured Schofield wouldn't dare kill De Chelly. Looks like I was wrong."

"Where's the draft?" Tom asked. "If you die, there won't be a shred of proof against Schofield without it."

In spite of his weakness, Durand managed to look crafty and proud. "You'll never guess."

"Damn you, I don't want to guess. I want to know."

"It's all in the confession booth at the Mission . . . stuffed into a crack on the right side about three feet from the floor."

Tom breathed a sigh. He had been so afraid Durand would die before he told where he'd hidden the draft.

For a while Durand lay still, his chest rising and falling weakly. Occasionally he coughed. At last he said: "You killed Stutz, didn't you, Tom?"

"Not exactly. We got in a fight and he fell on his own knife."

Durand grunted something that Tom didn't catch. Tom said: "What about Stutz? Where did he come in?"

"He was De Chelly's spy. He kept an eye on Schofield and kept tally on everything Schofield shipped. Without him, Schofield would have cheated us blind."

Tom's face twisted. What a sordid unsavory mess. Behind him he heard Miguel say softly: "*Amigo,* here they come."

Durand tried to sit up. He failed and sank back. His breathing now was almost inaudible. He said: "If you get out of here, Tom, talk to Bassett. He's your only chance." And then he died.

Tom didn't want to believe that he was dead. He laid his head on Durand's chest to listen for his heart. He heard nothing, and raised his head. He could see them coming now, vague shapes in the gathering darkness. They advanced in groups of four, one group rushing, while the other stayed prone on the ground, laying down a withering, covering fire. More bullets slammed into the corral, and more cattle went to the ground, kicking. Smelling blood, thoroughly confused and frightened, the remaining cattle charged from one side of the corral to the other, stopping occasionally to sniff and paw at their downed comrades.

Miguel, firing steadily with the Henry, said urgently: "*Compañero*, it is time to withdraw. In another few minutes they will be among us, and they outnumber us two to one."

Tom began to curse softly. But at last he said: "All right, Miguel. Get the horses ready. Load Maximiliano's body and take him and Gaspar with you back to Doc's place. Take Durand, too. But give me your rifle before you go. I'll cover you until you get clear."

Miguel did not protest. There was a brief flurry of movement behind Tom, who was firing at the advancing attackers. Gaspar groaned steadily from the pain of his leg wound, and screamed once as they loaded him upon a horse.

Tom kept watching for Schofield's burly shape, or Ziegler's skinny one, but he couldn't pick out either in the increasing darkness. He heard the horses move out behind him and enter the thicket. He stood up and began to reload. A fierce kind of joy sang in him, a savage anticipation. He whirled at a sound behind him.

"Come along, *amigo*," Miguel said. "It is not the time to die. Later tonight, perhaps, but not right now. Let them have these cattle. They wear our brand and can be found again. Let us return to McGuire's house, for they are sure to attack that next."

The fighting fever left Tom in a single, shuddering breath. Miguel was right. He holstered his revolver and hobbled toward his horse.

XVII

They rode back to the edge of the clearing, and, because Doc and Ivy were moving slowly with the wounded and dead, they paused to cover them and give them a start. Miguel led their two horses into the brush and tied them, then returned to lie prone on the ground beside Tom. Tom gave him his rifle, and Miguel opened up, trying to coax a few shots from the attackers so Tom would have something to shoot at.

He succeeded. Schofield and his men halted beside the corral and began to fire at the pair hidden at the edge of the brush. Tom fired quickly, offhandedly with the revolver, and was rewarded by a high yell of pain. After that, Schofield's men redoubled their fire.

Tom wished he could be sure of the man beside him, yet he knew he could not. Miguel would remain loyal only if it promised more profit than disloyalty. Miguel was a waiting enigma. He might help Tom defeat Schofield, but again he might turn on Tom and take this brush empire for himself.

"So I was right, *amigo*," Miguel murmured softly. "You killed Stutz, and then you and Doc buried him."

Tom muttered half angrily: "Damn it, I didn't kill him. He fell on his own knife."

He could sense Miguel's shrug. "What matter? He is dead. I listened to your talk with Durand. If you can prove all that was said, then everything Schofield has will belong to you."

"I hadn't thought of it, but I guess you're right."

"And where will Miguel Ortiz stand, *señor*? Will he still have a share in it all?"

"You'll get exactly what was promised you, neither more nor less."

Out in the clearing, the corral gate opened, and the cattle, urged by the high yells of Schofield's men, streamed out across the clearing and disappeared into the brush. Only wounded and dead animals remained within the corral. The herd was gone now.

Tom couldn't see Schofield, but he could hear the man's roaring bull voice. He felt a wildness taking hold of him. Schofield had killed Matt as surely as though he'd pulled the trigger himself. He had brazenly stolen Matt's place and begun to gather Matt's cattle along with whatever other animals he could find. When Tom had ridden in asking for a job, he'd had Tom beaten almost to death, and, because of Schofield, Tom had been framed for a killing he hadn't committed.

Suddenly nothing on earth seemed quite as important as getting Schofield. Tom pushed himself up and crouched, watching the scene out there.

He reloaded his gun by feel in the darkness, ignoring Miguel's query: "*¿Qué es, señor?* What are you doing?"

Schofield roared—"Bring up the horses!"—and Tom lunged to his feet.

Miguel clamped his hand on Tom's arm, gripping like an iron claw. "*Amigo,* don't be a fool! Schofield's men will kill you before you get a shot at the man himself!"

Tom tried to pull free, and then he heard the rapid beat of many hoofs. Next thing he knew, a cavalry patrol of over twenty men pounded into the clearing across the way.

Miguel pulled him back into the shelter of the brush. "Do you know what this means, *señor?* Schofield will point us out to the commander of that patrol. Then, while the patrol hunts us like animals through the thicket, Schofield and his men will ride back to Doc's place and burn it to the ground. You will be beaten, *señor,* just when things had begun to look as though you were going to win."

The patrol halted amidst a cloud of rising dust. Tom heard the commander's voice, arrogantly querying the men on the ground. The moon broke from a bank of clouds and illuminated the clearing. It drifted behind the clouds again, but Tom had seen enough. Hazel was not with the patrol. She had stayed at Doc's place.

He waited no longer. Lumbering clumsily because of his wounded leg, he lunged through the brush toward his horse. Miguel came after him.

For the first time since he'd been wounded, Tom slammed a foot into the stirrup and mounted normally. Knives of pain lanced his leg, but he gritted his teeth, and with a hard hand reined the horse around.

Behind him, he could hear the patrol coming. Then he was leaning low, eyes intent on the brush ahead, spurs gouging the frightened horse's sides. Miguel had been right, he knew. Schofield had simply pointed out his location at the edge of the brush. The cavalry patrol was in full pursuit, while Schofield and his men hung back to wait. Then with the cavalry patrol out of the way, they could ride to McGuire's.

His ears were full of the sounds of crackling brush, of horse's hoofs right behind him, of the yells of the patrol as they tore into the thicket. He heard one horse go down, thrashing wildly, and heard the cavalryman's scream as the full weight of horse and saddle crushed his body.

He resisted the impulse to look back. Suddenly a post oak loomed before him, its branches low enough to knock a man from his saddle. Tom left the saddle, squatting in a single stirrup on the horse's left side and clinging to his neck with an arm. The saddle horn struck the branch with an impact that threatened to shatter the saddle tree, and then the horse flashed past the oak, and Tom swung back into the saddle. He stifled a moan of agony. He yelled: "Miguel, look out!"

But for the cloud-shrouded moon and its grudging light, this brush riding at night would have been impossible. As it was, the odds against a man traveling a mile safely were twenty to one. Miguel must have ducked the branch successfully, for Tom heard no immediate crash behind him, and the closely pursuing hoof beats continued. A moment later, however, the patrol reached the oak.

Some of them must have reined around. Two or three did not. Tom heard the branch groan as they struck it, heard one of their horses fall, and roll end over end, shrilly neighing its terror.

The others came on, but they had now lost ground. "¡Hola, amigo!" Miguel shouted gleefully. "Ride!"

Tom struck a game trail and swung into it. Now he could increase his speed. He risked a look around and saw Miguel ten yards behind. The patrol was not yet in sight. Oddly Miguel began to slow up and fall behind.

The patrol swung into the trail, and their leader's revolver flared. The bullet cut brush six or eight feet from Tom's horse and off to his right. Tom swung out of the trail, charging directly into the choking brush.

Dodging brush forces any rider into zigzags and arcs that would strain a snake's spine, but somehow Tom held to a general course that would carry him to McGuire's. Although he dared not look around, he knew Miguel must still be losing ground. The sounds of Miguel's horse were dwindling rapidly.

What was Miguel up to? Was he deliberately hanging

back, intending to let Tom and Ivy and Doc take on Schofield and his crew? Did he intend to come in and mop up, taking what was left for himself?

Gradually the clouds had been thickening across the face of the moon, and now the night was nearly pitch black. Tom slowed, for the sounds of pursuit were almost gone. He scanned the sky. Lightning flashed along the horizon. Minutes later, thunder boomed dismally.

Tom's pants hung in shreds from the knees down. The bandage on his leg had been almost torn off. A thorn had pricked through it into his wound, and now, made conscious of it by increasing pain, he felt for it and yanked it free. His hat was gone. Blood trickled across his forehead and down one cheek from a thorn scratch almost the width of his forehead.

His horse was only trotting now, and blowing heavily. Tom reined him in and listened. He could hear nothing but that distant rumble of thunder upon the horizon, the uneasy stirring of brush in the rising wind. Had they caught Miguel? He shook his head. Impossible. Had Miguel led them off deliberately? He doubted it. Had Miguel deliberately lagged and gone off for purposes of his own? This was the likeliest possibility.

Tom kneed his horse into motion again. Maintaining a steady gait, he rode until he neared McGuire's. As he traveled, the wind increased. Black clouds scudded low overhead, riding the skies at unbelievable speeds. The lightning drew closer, probing the brush with its pointed, searching fingers as though pursuing a fleeing man. In the glare from these sheets of lightning, Tom could see the approaching wall of rain—a rare phenomenon, this, in the middle of winter. Usually winter rains were soft, steady showers that soaked the thicket and dripped from the branches to the thirsty ground. Storms such as this usually relieved the hot days of summer.

Lightning struck suddenly, not fifty yards away. It cracked and split, running along the ground in all directions. The hair on Tom's head and the hair on his horse's body stood straight up, glowing light blue with the charge it had absorbed. The horse reared, neighing shrilly. He came down, whirled, and would have bolted but for Tom's iron hand on the reins. Balked, the terrified animal began to buck.

Tom hung on, fighting a rising faintness caused by the incredible pain in his leg. The jolting continued until he thought his leg was being torn from his body. The world whirled and dimmed. Unconsciousness was like a gray curtain, slowly being lowered across his eyes. Quickly, then, he abandoned the saddle before he was thrown from it. He landed on both feet and let his legs collapse and rolled. The horse thundered away into the brush.

For a moment, Tom lay still. Then, shaking his head, he came to his knees. A damned good thing, he thought, that a man can get mad and stay that way. Otherwise he'd give up.

He got to his feet and stumbled through the thicket toward Doc's house. He was limping painfully, and several times he fell. The rain came down, sweeping across the thicket like a wall. It drenched him completely in less than a minute. Afterward, it beat into his face as though trying to push him back.

Time ran on, frighteningly fast. Would he reach the house in time? He felt for his revolver in sudden panic, and breathed a long sigh when he found it in its holster. At last, in a flare of lightning, he saw the huge house looming before him. Then the flash faded and everything was dark save for the feeble glow of lamplight shining from the kitchen window.

Tom crossed the clearing at a shambling run. Lightning flashed again and he looked through the torrential downpour toward the corral. He saw no horses there, which meant that Doc and Ivy had not yet arrived. Tom knew he must reload his gun, an impossibility here in the dark and rain. He burst through the kitchen door with it clutched in his hand.

Hazel looked up, her eyes lighting with relief. Then she saw his condition and ran toward him. He brushed her aside. "Get all the guns in the house and get them fast. Powder and caps and ball, too. Spread the stuff out here on the table."

He already had the Colt Navy dismounted, and he began loading the cylinder. He fished a spare from his pocket and loaded that, too.

Hazel came back, her arms loaded with an odd collection of antique firearms. "What happened?" she asked breathlessly.

"Schofield killed Durand and Maximiliano. Wounded Gaspar. The patrol you sent arrived and Schofield sicced them on Miguel and me. I know the way Schofield's mind works. He's figuring that patrol will chase Miguel and me through the thicket all night, giving him time to come here and burn the house."

He liked the way Hazel took the news. Her hands trembled slightly as she picked up a gun, but she went to work loading it. He wondered how Annemarie Bassett would have acted in a like situation, and had to smile. Annemarie would have been in hysterics by now, probably begging him to try to make a deal with Schofield.

Over the roar of the storm he heard the barn door slam.

He ran out, gun in hand. Doc was leading the horses into the barn. Tom said: "Not in there, Doc. Lead 'em up to the house so we can unload Durand and the others quicker."

Ivy and Doc each grabbed an extra horse, and Tom led the one that bore Durand's body. Drenched by the downpour, they slipped and slid across the muddy yard to the kitchen door, unloaded their inert burdens, and carried them inside. Hazel began to tend the wound in Gaspar's leg, which Doc had hastily bandaged out at the corral.

Again Tom wondered where Miguel had gone, and wished that he were here. He looked at Doc, gulping courage from a stoneware jug, and at Ivy, waiting his turn at the jug. Neither of them was going to be much help tonight. He crossed the room, seized the jug, and smashed it on the floor.

"Get on up to the front of the house," he said. "Pick yourselves a window and stay with it."

They took their sullen departure, scowling. They acted as if they didn't realize that tonight would see the final showdown between themselves and Schofield, but Tom thought they did. They just didn't like to face the idea. To them, a showdown spelled sure death.

Hazel finished with Gaspar, who was unconscious. She washed her hands in a pan of water and dried them with quick, nervous movements. She said: "We haven't much chance, have we, Tom?"

"Damned little. Schofield's got eight men. He's got to kill us all because we saw him kill Durand. Not only that, but he probably knows Durand talked." Quickly he told her all that Durand had said.

She stood before him, seeming smaller, seeming defenseless now, with her eyes so soft and wet. "Tom, kiss me before it starts. Give me something in case. . . ."

She didn't finish. Tom folded her in his arms, gently at first. Then he felt the contours of her body against him, and his arms tightened savagely, hungrily. She was crying when he let her go. She started to cross the room toward the window. She picked up a rifle as she passed the table.

A shot ripped through the window and *clanged* against the cast-iron stove like a sledge. Tom swung his hand fast, sending the lamp to the floor with a crash, but not before a second bullet crashed through the remains of the window.

Those shots must have been a signal, for they touched off a barrage that tore through the walls as though they were paper. Nor was it confined to the rear of the house. Less loudly, but just as deadly, a fusillade raked the front of the house. Almost immediately Doc and Ivy answered with their large-bore rifles.

Hazel crouched below the windowsill. Tom flung himself across the room and sent her rolling to the floor. He could not stand the idea of her being exposed to gunfire.

He raised himself above the windowsill just as lightning flashed outside, and in its glare he flung a shot at a man standing, spraddle-legged, at the edge of the brush. He saw the man go down before the flare of lightning died.

Where was Miguel, and where were the troops who had been pursuing him? Now he wished he had ridden slower and led the troops back here. But that would have done no good, either. Schofield would have simply waited until they hauled Tom off to town, and then gone ahead with his attack.

Tom eased himself up again, waiting for another lightning flash. He knew they hadn't a chance in the world of winning tonight. The only thing they could do was to make Schofield's victory as costly as possible.

XVIII

For a few minutes the exchange of shots continued, with no apparent casualties on either side, but the occupants of the house were fighting under a serious disadvantage and Tom knew it. They could not hope to cover all the windows, or even all the doors. It would not be too hard for Schofield's men to infiltrate into the house and take its defenders from behind. Or, if they liked the idea better, they could simply toss cans of coal oil into the windows and follow up with lighted matches. That might be what they were doing right now. Tom found himself listening intently for sounds within the house.

Schofield chose this particular moment to offer his surrender terms. From the direction of the barn he bellowed: "Cady! Listen good, because I ain't goin' to make the offer twice. Walk out here with your hands in the air an' no gun. Do that an' we'll let the rest of your outfit alone."

Tom looked at Hazel, although she was only a shadowy form in the darkness. "What do you think, Hazel? You think he might be telling the truth?"

"Tom, no! You can't go out there. He's not going to spare any of us. You know that."

"Yeah. I knew it. But I wanted to be sure you did, girl."

"Make up your mind!" Schofield bellowed. "I ain't goin' to wait all night!"

Tom yelled back—"Go to hell!"—and then said excitedly to Hazel: "He gave me an idea, by God. If I really was to go outside, maybe we'd have a chance."

"Alone? Don't be a fool, Tom."

"I'm not. We've got just exactly no chance at all the way things stand. But if I was to go out . . . hell, that's the last thing in the world they expect. It's raining buckets out there. Chances are they wouldn't know me from one of their own in that kind of a mess."

"Then I'll go with you."

"No, you won't. If you were out there, I'd be worrying about you every minute. I wouldn't be able to do a thing. You stay here and every once in a while shoot a gun out the window. But keep down when you do."

She stirred out of the shadows and came creeping across the floor to him. She eased herself up beside him and he felt her soft lips on his face. "Tom, if anything happens, I want you to know I love you. I want you to know I'm not afraid any more, or bitter, either. There was something I didn't know."

"What was that?"

"That, if you love someone and can share things with him, even ugly things become beautiful. Right now I think a one-room shack in the brush that was full of your children would be heaven."

He touched her face and found it wet. She began to tremble. He pushed himself away from her and got to his knees, strangely excited and strangely moved. "I'll be back," he said.

"Yes, Tom. Yes."

He crept farther back in the house, knowing that he could not go out the kitchen door without being seen. He went down the hallway, feeling along the wall until he came to a door. He recognized it as the door that led into a small sewing room. As good a place as any, he decided. He went in, threading his way carefully amongst the scattered pieces of furniture until he came to the window.

Now came the test. Could he raise the window sound-lessly enough so that it would not be heard by Schofield's men? He knew how the screech of an unused window can carry, but there was rain outside, and thunder. He checked the window to be sure the lock was off, then got a firm grip on it. A moment later lightning flashed. In its glare, he scanned the yard, seeing no one. He waited tensely for the roll of thunder to follow the lightning. When it came, he heaved on the window with all his strength. It screamed in protest, but the screech might have been lost in the roar of thunder.

He wasted no time in wondering. He eased himself through the window and dropped to the ground, favoring his hurt leg as he did. Rain came down in a sheet from the eaves of the house. He stood there, getting his bearings, holding his gun under his brush jacket to keep it dry. Then he moved out across the yard.

In his mind, he tried to place Schofield's men. He doubted if they'd dispersed or tried to enter the house as yet. They'd be in or near the barn, huddled against the cold, wet to the skin. Schofield must be waiting, waiting to see if anxiety, fear, and time wouldn't wear down the occupants of the house. Tom had no intention of tackling them all at once, but he wanted Schofield. If he could just get Schofield, his men would have nothing left to fight for.

Mud and water were inches deep under Tom's sliding feet. Rainwater ran in a river off his head and down his back inside his shirt. He hunched a little to protect the gun he held under his jacket and against his belly. Lightning caught him in the exact center of the yard. It flared off to his right a quarter of a mile. It faded quickly, but for the briefest instant it illuminated the yard in a glare that was bright as day.

He froze, and waited for the crack of rifles over there at the barn. Nothing happened, and then he saw them, huddled in the wide barn doorway. Two of them were up in the loft, looking down. He made a rough count, relieved. At least they had not dispersed. They were not yet trying to enter the house.

The lightning died. The thunder following it cracked so sharply that it made Cady wince. He ducked to the right and began to run, the sound of his footsteps in the mud seeming inordinately loud in the silence after the thunderclap.

Two or three orange flares blossomed in the barn doorway, followed immediately by their spiteful muzzle blasts. One of the bullets struck the ground ten feet to Cady's left and showered him with particles of mud. He swerved, and gained the corner of the barn. He could hear Schofield's angry voice: "Who was it? Cady? I couldn't make him out."

And Ziegler's deadly tones: "Yeah. It was Cady. Now, damn it, are you going to let me burn that house?"

"All right. Go ahead. We'll cover you in case the lightning strikes again."

Tom knew a moment of panic. Hazel was alone in the rear of the house. Doc and Ivy were both in the front. Once before Ziegler had tried to kill her. How would Ziegler go? Would he take a straight line across the yard? Or would he slip along the barn wall and cross to the brush, returning to the house only when he had put it between himself and the barn? Cady didn't know, and he couldn't afford to guess.

He slid along the barn wall, probing the darkness with slitted eyes. Rain poured off the barn roof in a veritable flood that occasionally struck his left shoulder with a noisy splash. Ziegler would be halfway to the house by now. Why didn't the lightning flash? Oh, God, why didn't the lightning flash?

Cady opened his mouth to call out, hoping either to halt Ziegler or to draw a shot from him. In that instant, the lightning struck. It struck the peak of the house roof, and ran along the slope of the roof, and then it jumped to the ground. In its wake it left a path of flame. Shingles, scattered as though by an explosion, rained down in the yard. Concussion and an odd kind of shock drove Tom back hard against the wall of the barn. But he saw Ziegler.

"Ziegler!"

Staggering, trying to run, Ziegler went to his knees. The face Tom glimpsed was white with shock. Tom Cady got his gun out from beneath the duck jacket in a split tenth of a second, but it came out too late. The flare of lightning died, and then the yard etched like a memory in Tom Cady's eyes.

Gradually his eyes adjusted themselves. He saw the flaming roof—and in the red glow of the flame the figure of Ziegler, struggling to his feet. Ziegler's body lengthened, then crouched. Its lean shape actually seemed to coil, like a rattler about to strike. His right hand blurred downward with a speed Tom would not have believed possible had he not witnessed it himself.

Ziegler's gun came up, blurring again like a whip in midair. Its muzzle flashed, and a bullet chunked into the barn wall at Tom's side. Tom fired with automatic precision, hardly realizing he was doing so. Three bullets left the muzzle of the gun before he saw Ziegler begin to fall.

With his vulnerability proven, Ziegler's stature seemed to desert him. He became, instead of a deadly snake-like monster, only a scarecrow figure to which clung a ragged assortment of dripping garments. Ziegler folded quietly to the mud and lay there with his head half submerged in a puddle, unmoving and still.

The shock effect of lightning striking so very close, followed immediately by the sight of the deadly Ziegler beaten and dying, held Schofield and his men immobile and saved Tom Cady's life.

Rain hissed as it struck the flaming roof of the house. It pelted the muddy, puddled ground with a cumulative sound that caused a steady roaring in Cady's ears. Wind sighed through the dripping brush and added its small part to the cacophony of the elements. Thunder muttered along the horizon, and occasionally rumbled closer and louder.

Tom Cady ran along the barn wall toward the corner and ducked behind it. From a corner of his eye he glimpsed Schofield and his men leaping from the door. Half a dozen shots racketed, but the bullets whined away, lost in space, striking nothing. Immediately Tom whirled and flung the remaining bullets in his gun at the group before the door. A man howled and fell, writhing in the mud. The others dragged him back inside. The man began to curse Cady steadily and with fluent obscenity.

Schofield's bellow carried from one end of the clearing to the other. "Out the back, god damn you! Get out the back door while he's coverin' the front!"

Tom dismantled the Colt Navy by feel in the darkness. He slipped the used cylinder out and inserted the spare, careful not to let any of the gun's parts slip from his hands. He knew Schofield's roar might well be for the purpose of luring him to the rear of the barn while they all slipped out the front. He knew, too, that he couldn't cover both exits. He decided to stand pat. The fire on the roof was dying, being extinguished by the torrential rain. Suddenly, out behind the barn, Cady heard two quick shots.

"Back inside, *señores!*" a familiar voice said. "Back inside, or Miguel Ortiz will blow your head off!"

A slow grin creased Tom Cady's face. He thumbed back the hammer on his gun and stepped away from the corner of the barn, beyond the cascading water that ran from the eaves. The rain was slowing now. The lightning and thunder were moving off into the distance. The fire was almost out on the roof, but a single tongue of flame still flickered in the hole torn there by the lightning bolt. By its dim, uncertain light, Tom saw the bulky form of Schofield come from the barn door.

This could be treachery. Schofield's men might be just behind him, sheltered by the darkness of the barn door, waiting until Schofield stood clear before cutting loose on Cady. Tom had no time to think about it. Schofield had seen him. Schofield's gun was falling into line.

Tom fired offhand, too quickly. He missed, and saw the flare from the muzzle of Schofield's gun before the report from his own faded from his ears. The bullet hit his shoulder and spun him half around. He whirled back crazily, flinging another off hand shot at Schofield, with better accuracy than before. He saw Schofield double over. The will of the man was terrific. He straightened, his face a mask of concentration, and pointed his gun at Cady. Weakness was creeping into Cady's mind. The gun in his hand seemed to weigh 100 pounds. He lifted it with an effort and squeezed the trigger.

Schofield staggered back, his throat streaming blood, but from a sitting position he raised his gun again. It reminded Tom of a time in his youth, of a hog he and his father intended to butcher. The hog had refused to die, although stunned with a club, its throat cut, and a bullet in its skull. Schofield's gun bellowed, and Tom returned the shot. He saw water mist away like dust from the spot on Schofield's coat where the bullet struck. At last, Schofield began to fold. From his sitting position he slowly slid over sideways. His hat fell off and his head settled silently into the mud. Yet even in death there was vitality in the man, a refusal to be beaten. His hand tightened on his gun, and the gun, its muzzle buried in mud, exploded, sending its parts flying everywhere.

For a moment, Tom was stunned. Then he became aware of someone beside him. "*¡Señores!*" Miguel was shouting. "*Señores,* the game is up! Toss your guns out the door! Would you now die for a man who is dead? Toss your guns out and perhaps we may let you go!"

Tom lost interest in the proceedings. He started for the house as the clouds broke overhead and let the glow of the moon's light through. Hazel burst from the kitchen door, running toward him.

A patrol of cavalry skidded into the yard, enveloped in their gutta-percha rain capes. Tom whirled, ready to do battle with them all, but a voice came out, Silas Bassett's voice, ordering harshly: "Hold your fire, Cady! Hold on!"

Bassett stood spread-legged in the rain and demanded irritably: "What the hell's this all about? Can't you people live around here without killing each other?"

Tom stared at him silently. Hazel stood at his side and told Bassett in a few clipped sentences all that had happened since Tom's return from the war. She also told him of the death of Matt Cady, the incidents which had led to it, and the later developments. When she finished, she glared spiritedly at Bassett.

"You're not taking him to jail, either," she said. "He's done nothing that any man wouldn't do in like circumstances."

Bassett smiled at her, and his voice was strangely gentle. "No. I'll not be taking him to jail. You put him to bed, young lady, and take good care of him." He looked at Tom. "You don't even want a man to earn his pay, do you? How do you think my report is going to look? You've done all the work and all that's left for me is to cart off the bodies."

Tom wanted to find a bed and lie down on it. It had been a rough time, but now it was over. He'd better get busy healing his wounds and gaining strength. He looked down at Hazel. Her radiant, brimming eyes told him that now at last she had all the security she would ever want.

SUNDOWN

I

Arriola was a cheerless town in winter. Cottonwoods made their naked tracery against the gray sky. Snow, dirtied by the dust and smoke, accumulated in spots sheltered from the sun. The town's business houses all needed paint, all needed their windows washed. At only three spots on Main was there sign of activity, these three being the two saloons and Samson's store. In the exact center of the street before Samson's, a windmill spun dizzily in the strong, cold wind. From its discharge pipe a steady stream of water splashed into the tank at the windmill's base.

Lew Atkins left Samson's and mounted his horse. He pointed the animal south out of town. Under his wide-brimmed hat, a brown wool muffler came down over his ears and tied under his chin. The collar of his worn sheepskin was turned up against the bitter wind that pelted him from behind with the flakes of stinging snow.

When he saw Abe Healy's wagon on the road entering town, he reined over to the rail, swung down, and fished under his coat for the makings. It was not the cold entirely that made his fingers like thumbs as he tried to separate a single paper from the pack. He managed it, but his fingers trembled noticeably as he shook flake tobacco into the tiny trough of paper. He licked the cigarette, sealed it, and stuck it between his firm lips. He raked a match alight on the rough surface of his sheepskin. Cupping his hands around

179

it, he touched it to the cigarette tip and raised his eyes to stare over the flame.

She sat beside her husband, her fine shoulders defiantly straight. Her eyes were fixed steadily on a rosette in the breeching straps. There was a blue bruise on her cheek bone that had not been there the last time Lew saw her. Her color was high, but Lew could not have said whether that was caused by the long ride in the cold wind, or because she had seen him. Little Abby, five, subdued and silent, sat wrapped in blankets in the back of the wagon and cuddled a dirty doll.

Lew straightened as the wagon drew abreast, and with a full-armed swing threw the match into the street. The gesture was more expressive than he knew. It summed up his frustration and his anger. His eyes narrowed and grew cold. His mouth was almost ugly, the lips thinned hard against his even teeth.

The wagon went past him. Lew did not have to look at her any more. He had memorized each small feature of her face, from the full but pale lips, to the eyes, so resigned now, so filled with quiet acceptance. If Lew closed his eyes, he could still see the sweet curve of her cheek, the proud column of her throat, the soft midnight hair brushed back into a demure bun on her neck. But she was like a train on a steel track. There were no turn-offs, and few stops, only continuation to a predetermined end.

Lew himself was on another track, paralleling hers but never joining it. There was murder in his glance now as it rested on the broad, muscled back of Abe Healy. He was trembling visibly with the effort he made at holding himself in. It was almost as if the town did not exist, nor the people in it. It was as if the world consisted of these four—himself, Susan, Abby, and Abe Healy—and the trouble making up for them.

Phil Straight's quiet voice spoke at Lew's elbow. "It's a damned shame. But the time is coming when we'll get the goods on him and stretch a rope with his rotten carcass."

Lew swung around, anger plain in his slate-gray eyes. But Phil's glance was steady, saying no more than his words had said. Lew thought he knew what Phil was thinking: *We'll hang Healy, and then you can have his woman.* Or perhaps Phil wasn't thinking that at all. Perhaps Lew had got to the point where he assumed people were thinking what he thought they ought to be thinking.

Lew said: "You've got to get something on him before you can hang him, and you'll never do it. He's too blamed sly and he's got all the back-stabbing homesteaders on the flat helping him, or at least acting as lookouts for him. A cowman can't get to within five miles of his place but what he knows it."

Phil Straight looked away from him. Phil was a thin, graying man, a man who had earned the respect of all who knew him. Again Lew caught himself guessing the thoughts in Phil's head that would be: *You can, Lew. Otherwise, how did you get to know his wife?*

Lew tossed his cigarette onto the windswept boardwalk. Little whorls of sifting snow eddied briefly around it. Phil Straight stared at his scowling countenance for a moment, then shrugged lightly, turned away, and went into the saloon.

Upstreet, Abe Healy drew his team to a halt before Samson's store. Susan climbed down, then raised her arms to Abby, standing in the back. Susan's coat was shabby and thin. She was shivering. She stood for a moment, talking to Abe, and then climbed the steps to the walk before Samson's store. Her brief hesitation at the door told Lew as plainly as words could have done that Abe had given her no money, that she hated going inside with no slight excuse to justify her presence there. Lew would have bet that she didn't even have enough to buy Abby a sack of candy.

Abe drove the wagon to the far end of the street and, without unhitching, tied the team to a cottonwood. Lew knew why he never unhitched. By nightfall he'd be so drunk he wouldn't be able to tell the bridles from the breeching. Abe turned away from the wagon and walked downstreet. He went into the door at Solomon's, which was the farmers' saloon.

Lew jerked himself erect and took a step toward Samson's store. He halted himself at once. It wouldn't do. It just wouldn't do. By seeing her he only made things harder for her. He swung around and went into the Stockman's saloon. He got a bottle and glass at the bar and carried them to a table against the wall.

It had been a day something like this when he had first ridden into Healy's place almost a year ago. His horse had thrown a shoe over in the Black Cañon country where he'd been riding. He'd seen Healy's ramshackle layout in the distance and had ridden that way to borrow a horse. Healy had been gone. Lew supposed now that he had been driving a small bunch of stolen cattle toward the placers in the mountains. His wife had come to the door as Lew rode in.

Fear was the first emotion he saw in her, fear that widened her violet eyes, that made her full lower lip tremble ever so slightly. Little Abby peered around her mother, clutching her skirts, also afraid.

Lew nodded his head toward his horse. "He's thrown a shoe, ma'am, and gone lame. I was wondering if you'd have a horse I could borrow. I'm Lew Atkins, from over on the north fork of the Blue. I could return him tomorrow."

Lew hadn't shaved for a week. He was dirty from a

week's riding in a waterless country. He guessed he couldn't blame her much for her fear. But that was before he knew that fear was her daily companion.

"Well, I don't know. My husband. . . ."

"Isn't he here?"

"He's due back any minute." But for the woman's obvious fear, Lew would have smiled at this, so plainly was it untrue. He thought of how long would be the walk from there home. He decided suddenly that it would be silly to talk when this woman had two horses idling in her corral. He said: "Do you mind if I wait?"

"Well, I don't know. I. . . ."

Lew grinned at her, liking her and wondering why. She was pale and shabbily dressed. Her fear did not improve her looks, yet there was something about her. He said: "I'll wait out here. Don't be afraid of me. I've been riding for a week, and there's no water this time of year where I've been. Just snow, and a man can't wash in that."

He led his horse out to the corral and tied him. Then he hunkered down and rolled a smoke. He looked around the yard. There was a cellar not far from him, dug part way into the ground and sodded over the top. The door swung ajar at the foot of a short flight of dirt steps. *Empty*, thought Lew.

The house was like half a hundred homestead shacks on the high plains, hastily constructed, soon to be abandoned. A half-hearted attempt had been made to cultivate a twenty- or thirty-acre patch on the east side of the house, but apparently that had been abandoned before the plowing was finished. Lew could see the remains of a summer garden immediately in front of the house, but even that was gone, and from the tracks in it Lew assumed that cattle or horses had eaten it. He could almost imagine the woman pleading with her shiftless husband to fence in her garden, could guess at her anger and heartbreak on the morning she had come out and found it trampled and browsed down to the ground.

Lew felt briefly sorry for the woman. She did not look the type to starve and suffer and break her heart over a piece of land that would never amount to anything, over a husband who didn't even care enough to finish the plowing he had started. There had been a moderately bloody range war in this country two years before. The homesteaders had won it, had moved out onto the high plains to stake their claims. Undoubtedly this man was one of those. But he wouldn't stay. None of them stayed, because the land wouldn't support them.

Nearly a dozen cigarette butts littered the ground around Lew's feet before the door opened and the woman came out. The little girl hung back, staring at him from the open doorway. Lew got up and strolled toward Healy's wife.

She said, hesitant and a little ashamed: "I was afraid of you. My husband won't be back today. I . . . I guess you could take a horse. But would you bring him back tomorrow . . . in the morning? I don't know if Abe would like my loaning him, particularly to a cowman."

Lew smiled at her. He was cold from the blast of raw wind and he showed it.

The woman said: "I'm Susan Healy. You look awfully cold. Will you come in and have some dinner before you go?"

Lew accepted gratefully. The fare was plain, but it was filling. Beans and coffee made from scorched beans. Bread without butter.

Lew suddenly noticed the bruise that darkened the

woman's left eye. It was apparently almost healed, which was why he had not noticed it before. To make conversation, he asked politely: "You have a fall, ma'am? That's a nasty bruise on your eye."

Her instant confusion, the flush that raced into her face gave Lew his answer. He flushed himself and dropped his glance to his plate. Little Abby piped: "Daddy did it. Didn't he, Ma?"

Lew looked up. He murmured: "I'm sorry. I was just trying to make talk." But he could feel his first anger rising then. What was the matter with a man that would hit a woman like this one?

He finished his beans, thanked Mrs. Healy, and got up. He petted little Abby's smooth hair awkwardly as he went toward the door. "Any special horse I should take?"

"No. Either one is all right. You will bring him back tomorrow, won't you?"

"You count on it," said Lew, and closed the door behind him. He tramped across the yard toward the corral. He turned his own horse loose, knowing the animal would find his own way home within twenty-four hours, and saddled one of those in the corral, a bald-faced roan.

As he rode, he tried to remember Healy. If the man had been there at the time of the fracas between cowmen and homesteaders, he knew he should remember him. Healy. The name had a familiar ring.

Lew had been one of the cowmen who had urged moderation in the trouble. "Let them settle," he'd said. "Why make criminals out of ourselves doing what Nature will do for us?"

Lew's counsel had not prevailed. There had been a rash of homestead burnings, a couple of killings. But the homesteaders came too fast. A handful of cowmen couldn't burn them all out, or fight them once they got organized. The cowmen's resistance had finally collapsed. And time had proved Lew Atkins right. The first year had seen a drought that withered the nesters' crops. The second summer had been fine right up to the 1st of June. Then the crops had withered again, for not a drop of rain fell from then on, and the weather turned blistering hot and stayed that way.

II

That fall had seen a general exodus. Homesteaders packed up and left by the hundreds. Thereafter cattle grazed their fields. But a small, hard core of the stubborn were still left. Men like Healy. Men who had no place to go, who had not the ambition to go if they had. Men who were not above the rustling of a few head of some cowman's steers to keep them in whiskey and beans.

Starting small, the thing had snowballed, until it had become a very real source of concern to the cowmen. The nesters were smart and so far they had avoided being greedy. They trailed their cattle in weather that was sure to hide their tracks, in snow and rain and wind. They had a system of lookouts that was unbeatable.

Lew dismounted at his own place and put the borrowed roan into the barn. He threw down a few forkfuls of hay and, from the way the horse picked at it, knew he was unfamiliar with hay.

Lew's place nestled in a kind of hollow, back to the north, so that the bitter winter winds were broken by the time they struck it. A spring welled out of the ground behind the house, trickled past it to drip into a tank in the center of the corral. The house itself was long and low, built of spruce logs, that Lew had freighted from the mountains fifteen miles away, and chinked with adobe mud. There was a stone fireplace and chimney that also attested to Lew's industry, for there was not a rock closer than five miles.

Lew went inside and kindled a fire in the stove. He fried some steaks and potatoes and boiled some coffee. Perhaps in his thinking and his loneliness that night had begun his attraction to Healy's wife. Perhaps it was something else, the natural resentment a man feels at seeing any pretty woman mistreated. Whatever it was, he found himself thinking of her as he tossed on his bed, found that she was first in his thoughts the following morning. It was with a real feeling of anticipation that he mounted and, trailing the borrowed roan, rode out just after sunrise.

Shaved and washed, Lew made a different picture as he rode into Healy's yard the second time. He was a big man, young and strongly muscled. He had a young man's seeming indolence of posture, yet behind this there was nervous intensity and energy that was boundless. The planes of his face were hard and flat, and his eyes showed the world that he had known his hard times, had known bitterness and failure. But they showed as well an irrepressible humor and a readiness to smile.

He turned the roan into the corral, tied his own horse, and tramped toward the house. Susan came to the door, smiling, and Lew realized then that it was the first time he had seen her smile. There was shy reserve in the smile, and uncertainty, but it was a smile.

Little Abby peered around her skirt, reminding Lew of a puppy, tail wagging and yearning for affection, yet half fearing a blow or a curse.

Some inner prompting told Lew forcefully then: *Thank her and get out of here. And don't come back.* Susan Healy seemed less shabby this morning, but it did not occur to Lew that she had dug her once-good dress out of the trunk and put it on. She said, still smiling: "Thank you for bringing him back so early." She did not ask Lew in, and a sudden shyness showed in her violet eyes.

Looking at her, Lew suddenly realized that she was truly beautiful. Her features had a fine regularity. Her nose and mouth were generous. Yet it seemed to be more than simple beauty of face and form. There was an inner beauty that shone from Susan Healy, beauty that stemmed from character. She colored at Lew's steady stare.

He flushed and lowered his glance. He said: "You saved me a long walk by the loan of that horse. I'm obliged. If I can return the favor. . . ."

There was nothing more to be said. In them both was the full consciousness that Susan was a married woman, which neither would acknowledge nor admit. Susan's smile was fading. Her eyes were wide and vulnerable. Lew took a step toward her, and fright suddenly leaped from their violet depths. She said shortly: "It's all right. You were welcome." She hesitated only another instant, and then she said: "Good bye." She closed the door.

Lew stood for an instant where he was. There was the vaguest sort of disappointment in him, but, as he turned away, he admitted: *She's right, of course.* Yet he could not forget the vulnerability of her eyes, nor could he brush aside the very real attraction that had been so plain between them. Heading for the corral, he tried to convince himself that he had imagined it, which indeed was possible since by neither word nor action had she been less than she should have been. Yet between man and woman at times there passes a current, a current of attraction that needs no words or actions. It is unmistakable, undeniable.

Stirred by vague and helpless anger, Lew mounted and swung toward the house. He caught a flash of white at the window, knowing instantly that she had been watching him. Excitement stirred his blood, but he went on past the house and took the long trail toward home.

Weeks passed. He worried about her and he wondered about her, could not forget her. A dozen times he started to ride over and see her, but each time he was stopped before he had gone a mile by a feeling of guilt. She was Abe Healy's wife. That was an incontrovertible fact. She was another man's wife, and respect for the sanctity of marriage was as ingrained in Lew as his honesty or his courage.

Pure accident brought about their third meeting, on the road to Arriola in early spring. Riding along alone, Lew suddenly came around a shaly outcropping and there she was, she and little Abby alone. The wagon they had been riding was canted at an angle against the road, and a wheel lay beside it, broken off at the axle. Lew rode up, unsmiling, excitement and yearning churning in his heart. "Trouble?"

She had been crying. She dabbed at her eyes. Her face was smudged with grease from the axle. Her hands were dirty and her dress was torn. She had apparently tried to lift the wagon by herself. She said helplessly: "I tried to fix it, but I'm not strong enough. I guess I couldn't have fixed it anyway. It's broken off."

Lew dismounted. He knelt to look at the broken axle. A vague aura of woman fragrance drifted into his nostrils. He looked up at once. She was kneeling, too, looking at the broken axle and the furrow it had plowed in the hard-packed road. Abby had wandered off to the side of the road, chasing one of the tiny, fast desert lizards.

Susan looked up, feeling Lew's glance upon her, and

their eyes locked desperately. Lew stood up. He reached down his hands to help her to her feet.

It was the first time he had touched her. Even through the thickness of dress and coat, the touch was electric. For a timeless instant he stared into her eyes, his hands tightening on her arms. Nothing existed in the world but man and woman. He could recall no movement, no movement at all. But she was in his arms, hard-pressed against him. His lips were against hers. She cried—"No! Oh, no!"—and fought away. He let her go, although soaring fire seared his brain.

No longer was it just the two of them and Abby playing in the weeds at the side of the road. There was a fourth presence here, that of Abe Healy.

Lew said: "I'm sorry, Susan. Not sorry that I kissed you, but sorry that I didn't find you first. Do you know how much I've wanted to ride over and see you?"

She nodded, looking at the ground. "Perhaps I do. Perhaps I wanted you to. But you mustn't ever do it. Not ever." She raised her face to him. There was a suspicious shine in her eyes. "Will you send out an axle from town?" She hesitated briefly, flushing slowly and painfully. "No. Don't do that. I have no money."

Not looking at Lew, she went to the side of the road and caught Abby up by her hand. Leading the child, and still not looking at Lew, she walked back up the road toward Healy's homestead shack.

In this instant an undying hatred for Abe Healy was born in Lew. Abby wailed: "Mama, do we got to walk?" Lew swung up to his saddle and trotted after them. When he reached Susan, he swung down and, leading his horse, fell into step beside her. He said: "You helped me once. Won't you let me return the favor?"

"After what has happened?" Her words in themselves

were a reproof, yet there was nothing of reproof in her glance.

He said roughly: "You can't walk all the way home. It's over ten miles. You'd be carrying the little girl before you'd gone two."

"It's the only way."

"No. Let me help you. I won't touch you again."

She did not slacken her pace. Abby had to skip to keep up with her. Lew felt his anger rise. He said: "Hang it, I'd do as much for any woman I met on the road. Any man would do what I want to do for you. Don't be a fool, Susan!"

There was a certain ridiculousness about this that did not escape Lew. Apparently now Susan saw it for the first time. She stopped. "This is rather silly, isn't it? All right. We'll wait at the wagon. But whatever is needed, charge it to my husband. That is only right."

"All right." Lew rode away quickly. He knew that if he stayed they would both be sorry.

Riding, he puzzled over this. What was it about her that had so enslaved him in three short meetings? Was it because he pitied her? He shook his head. Was it simple anger because she did not deserve the humiliation and abuse that was her lot? Was it love, or was it only a lonely man's desire for a woman who he sensed had much to give?

Scowling, Lew shook his head. He stopped at the livery barn and told the hostler to send out a rig after Susan and Abby. Then he stopped at the blacksmith shop and asked Hugh Neff to drive out and replace the broken axle. "If Healy don't pay it, Hugh, let me know and I will."

Then he took the long trail back to his ranch.

III

Lew Atkins welcomed spring and summer, welcomed the calf branding, the sweat, the blood, and stink of burning hair. He welcomed the aching tiredness that crept into his bones and stayed. He welcomed the hard jerk of a full-grown steer hitting the end of his rope.

Although there was no real need for it, he punished himself deliberately, staying in the saddle fourteen hours a day, so that, when he hit his bedroll, he dropped off to sleep immediately from numbed exhaustion. It was the only way he could live with himself. Yet even with this self-punishment, he still had time to think of Susan. And he caught himself thinking of murder.

He lost weight. He grew irritable and short-tempered. He even put his ranch on the market, and tried to sell it. But the cattle market fell through the summer, and continued to fall as shipping time grew near, and the ranch found no buyers.

Lew fought continually with the desire to see her again, if only to look at her, to see how she was, if well, or ill, if happy or as miserable as he was himself. He planned rides that would take him within a few miles of Healy's shack, always abandoning them as quickly as he realized what he was doing.

As midsummer eliminated the need for day-long riding, he freighted logs from the mountains and built himself a barn. He dug a root cellar and walled it with stone, hauled on a stone boat from a sandstone quarry five miles distant. He fenced and repaired his corral. At last, in desperation, he went to Arriola and the Stockman's saloon. He got drunk and stayed that way for a week.

He saw her face in the strangest places, on the round, white face of the moon at night, in the clear, rippling water of the creek at the edge of town, in the dark lobby of the hotel in early morning. Finally he decided: *I've got to go away, or I've got to see her.*

He spent a full day sobering up. His hands were shaky as he shaved, and he cut himself three times. He went to Samson's store and bought himself a new pair of jeans and a flannel shirt. With these on, he found his horse at the livery barn, saddled, and rode away.

It was early fall. Grass on the prairie was dry and long. It waved in the wind like wheat, a fascinating, rippling, ever-changing movement. Lew called himself a fool. He cursed himself long and bitterly. What did he hope to accomplish today? Did he think he could find a solution to this by seeing Susan?

He shook his head bitterly. Except for that one kiss, for the irresistible attraction they both felt, there was nothing between them. But he had never asked her. Today he would discard his old-fashioned notions that marriage was sacred. What was sacred about union with a man who was brutal and selfish, who beat his wife with his fists, who made living terror for his small daughter? What was sacred about marriage with a man who was dishonest, who inevitably would decorate a gallows and leave his wife and daughter penniless behind? And supposing Healy was at home? What would Lew say? He knew suddenly that, if Abe Healy was at home, he would simply turn around and ride away. Not that he was afraid to face the man. He would have welcomed that. But if Healy so much as suspected his interest in Susan, he would make life a living hell for her.

Suddenly Lew reined in. He turned his glance inward, and he did not like what he saw. This was no tawdry affair, yet it had that appearance. Hesitating, he held his horse still in the road. Stubbornness firmed out his lips. He went on. He left his horse behind a low rise and crawled to the top, to peer down at Healy's shack.

For half an hour he lay in the warm autumn sunlight and stared down. A light smoke plume climbed from the tin chimney. Abby played in the soft dust before the door. The corral was empty.

Finally Susan came out, carrying a basket of clothes that she began to hang on the sagging clothesline. Otherwise, not even a chicken stirred. A hawk wheeled overhead, giving the yard a brief inspection, and then soaring away.

Satisfied at last, Lew crawled back from the knoll, found his horse, and mounted. He rode down the slope.

Susan looked up. For the barest instant there was gladness and pleasure in her face, but it quickly faded. She said as he rode close: "Please! Please go away. I don't want to see you. I don't want to talk to you. I'm Abe's wife, and I'll not. . . ."

Lew's voice was harsh. "Nobody's asking you to do anything wrong. I'll give you some money. Go away. Go to Denver, to Santa Fé, or Cheyenne. Get a divorce from him. Then write to me and I'll come for you." He could see it was no good. All the sordid tales of desertion she had ever heard were plainly running through her mind. He said urgently: "God, Susan, I love you. It doesn't have to be a thing that you're ashamed of. There is nothing in your marriage contract that says he can beat you with his fists, that says he can spend everything he makes on liquor while you and Abby go hungry."

He stayed on his horse when every instinct within him told him to get down, to take her in his arms. Yet this would have been unfair. If love was as strong in her as it

194

was in him, her resolve would melt, and she would hate him later because he had made her betray her beliefs. Her decision must come from a clear head, or it would be no good.

He said: "I've thought of nothing but you for months. I can't sleep and I can't work. I've even thought of. . . ."

"What have you thought of, Lew?"

"Nothing." The full ugliness of what he had thought suddenly struck him. And Susan knew. He could tell that she knew. Her eyes widened. Lew asked hoarsely: "Will you do it? Will you do it, Susan?"

She shook her head. "No." She tried to smile. "I think you knew what my answer would be, didn't you, Lew? And I think you know why."

A perverse streak of stubbornness made Lew ask: "Why?"

Susan murmured, looking at the ground: "Marriage is not a thing to be discarded because things do not go right. Abe is the man I married. Perhaps he needs me more now than he did when I married him. Should I desert him because something better comes along for me?"

Lew's shoulders drooped. He had expected no more than this. He said softly: "I had to ask, Susan."

"I know. And I'm glad that you did. It will be something for me to remember." Her eyes sparkled with tears. Lew made a move to dismount, but she backed away. "No, Lew!"

"All right." He looked at her for a moment more. Abby came from her playing and smiled at him shyly. Lew said— "Good bye, Abby."—but the girl did not answer. She buried her face in Susan's skirt.

Lew whirled his horse and rode away. He looked back as he left the yard. Susan stood very straight, her dress molded around her body by the wind. She raised an arm and waved, but Lew did not wave back.

That was the way it had gone. Lew sat at his solitary table in the Stockman's saloon at Arriola and stared at the bottle and glass before him. He raised the brimming glass to his lips, but tonight just the smell of the liquor brought waves of nausea to his stomach. He set it down again.

Phil Straight came toward him and Lew looked up, scowling. Phil said: "Roundup tally showed my gather about a hundred and fifteen steers short. That's too many, Lew. It's going to make living pretty slim next year." He pulled out a chair and straddled it, folding his chin on his arms. "How did your count come out?"

Lew jerked his mind out of the past, forced it to concentrate on Straight and his question. He said finally: "About sixty, I guess. All steers."

"Well, it's the same all over. Joe Weems is out about twenty, and Joe has seven kids and a big mortgage at the bank. Woolery's out over two hundred. I guess he's the only one that can really afford the loss, but he ain't any happier about it than the rest of us. But you notice one thing, don't you? It's steers we're out. You see what that adds up to?"

"About four hundred cattle, all steers. It adds up to a pretty persistent bunch of rustlers. It adds up to a lot of meat over at the placers in the mountains . . . and a lot of buried hides."

Straight said: "And Abe Healy's spending gold eagles at Solomon's saloon. You know as well as I do that he hasn't made a crop in the three years he's been here. He hasn't worked, either."

Lew felt quick impatience. He shrugged. "Do something about him, then. Don't come crying to me."

"You're in it, too, Lew. You been staying pretty much to yourself the last year. But you're one of us. If we hope to make a stand, we all got to do it together. Because there's an army of bushwhacking homesteaders on the flats, and, if we don't do something now, next year they'll clean us out."

"What do you want to do?"

"Why, set a watch, I suppose. Take turns at it. None of us has got much crew this time of year, so we'll have to do it ourselves. There's only half a dozen ways Abe can drive cattle into the mountains. If we keep at it, we're sure to catch him sooner or later."

"Then what?"

Straight was normally a mild, genial man. But there was nothing mild about him now. His eyes were as cold as the winter sky. His voice was short and clipped. "Hang him. Make an example of him." Straight thumbed his hat back on his head. His forehead carried a red mark where the sweatband had been. Above that, his thinning hair was damp with sweat and plastered against his forehead.

"What about going to the law?"

"You know what the law in Arriola is, Lew. You know the sheriff's owned lock, stock, and barrel by the home-steaders."

Another man detached himself from the crowd at the bar and came diffidently toward the pair. This was Hugh Neff, the blacksmith, short and bald, still clad in leather apron and vest. His skin was ruddy and flushed, partly from the liquor he had consumed, partly from a lifetime of glowing forges. He hesitated half a dozen feet from the table, and Lew nodded to him. "Hello, Hugh. What's on your mind?"

"I guess I should forget it, Lew, but Nellie won't let me." His voice was hoarse, and he stopped to clear his throat.

Lew asked: "Forget what?"

"That wagon axle, Lew. You said if Healy didn't pay,

you would. He ain't paid it, Lew. I dunned him half a dozen times."

Straight was looking at Lew curiously. Lew could feel the unwilling flush climbing to his face. It gave him away. Without the flush, he might have passed it off, but now he couldn't.

He fished in his pocket. "How much was it, Hugh?"

"Four and a half, countin' the trip out there and a quarter for the kid I took along to drive their wagon to town."

Lew handed him a five.

Hugh rumbled: "I know it ain't your bill, Lew, but you said. . . ."

"Forget it."

Hugh shuffled back to the bar. Straight looked at Lew quizzically. "What was that about? You paying Healy's bills for him nowadays?"

Lew sighed. He tried to make his voice sound patient and resigned. "I came on his wife and kid just out of town last spring. The wagon was broke down and they didn't have any money. I sent Hugh out to fix them up and told him, if Healy didn't pay, I would."

Straight smiled. "She's a pretty woman, isn't she, Lew?"

Lew said: "Shut up! She's a married woman, and she isn't the kind. . . ."

"Whoa, now, Lew! Slow down. I didn't say anything. What's eatin' on you?"

Lew said: "I don't know, Phil. I don't know."

Phil murmured: "I've been your friend for a good many years, Lew. I'm about to give you some advice. If you don't want it, or if it will make you mad, tell me now and I won't give it to you."

Lew looked at the man. Straight was old enough to be

Lew's father. He was sober and friendly, and very serious. His brown eyes, with crow's feet of humor at their corners, were full of kindness and concern. Lew muttered: "Go ahead, Phil."

"Well, it's just this. You're ruining yourself. You tried killing yourself with work, and, when you couldn't do that, you tried liquor. I ain't saying Susan Healy isn't a fine woman. She is. But she ain't yours, Lew, and you can't make her yours."

Lew sat very still. It seemed to him that, if he moved a muscle, he would give himself away. He wanted to hit Phil. He wanted to fling the bottle through the big backbar mirror. After a full minute this way, he said: "So you know. Does the whole town know?" There was bitterness in his voice.

"I don't think they do, but, Lew, what's in it for you? She's a virtuous woman, or I'm no judge. Forget her."

"Forget her!" Lew's words were a sardonic curse. He looked at Phil, his eyes blazing. "Don't you think I've tried?" He got to his feet. "Do you see now why I don't want any part of catching Healy? He can steal every steer I own, and I still can't do anything. If I was involved in his killing, do you think she would look at me? I guess I hate Abe Healy more than a man ought to hate anything, but I can't do anything about it. I want to beat him with my fists. I want to close his eyes, ram his teeth down his throat, and break his jaw. I want to teach him how Susan feels when his damned fist crashes into her face. But if I lay a hand on him, then he'll know, and he'll take it out on her." His hands gripped the table edge as though he wanted to tear it apart. His voice was vicious, soft. "I want to kill him, but I can't!"

Straight whistled. "Boy, you've got it bad."

"Yeah, I guess I have." Lew stood up. He scowled at Straight, turned, and strode to the door. He banged it open and stepped onto the walk. The snow had thickened, but it still slanted horizontally, driven by a gale-size wind. Early dusk was upon the town, sundown on any ordinary day, deep, sober, gray.

Lamps winked in the recesses of some of the stores, putting a feeble glow on their clouded front windows, and smoke whipped away from chimneys as clouds of driven snow whirled down the street. Lew's horse had turned its rump to the wind, with tail whipped between its legs. The animal nickered at Lew.

Lew thought of Susan and Abby, forced to ride the twelve miles home yet tonight on the exposed wagon seat with drunken Abe Healy at the reins. He said—"Damn!"— and untied his horse from the rail. He turned his sheepskin collar up and swung to the saddle. Then he took the road toward home.

He had forgotten to wear gloves today, and his hand, holding the reins, turned numb. He alternated with the other, warming one all the time in his pocket. His mind was busy with his eternal problem.

He began to figure the extent of what the rustlers had gotten away with in the last year. 400 cattle. Conservatively priced, they still amounted to $12,000 or $15,000. Lew suspected that Abe Healy was the guiding force behind the rustling. So he would probably take at least half of the money for himself. He never gave his family anything. He spent nothing himself except for his liquor, and no man could drink up more than a small fraction of $6,000 in the amount of time Healy was in town. It followed, therefore, that Healy still had most of the money, probably over $5,000. A tidy sum. A devil of a lot of money. Why was he hanging onto it so desperately? Most men would have seen to it that their families were better provided for. Most men would have had some of the good things themselves.

For an instant, hope leaped in Lew's heart. He came to the fork in the road, and out of impulse paused. The right fork went on to Healy's homestead, forking at other places along the way to serve other homesteads, some abandoned, some occupied by die-hards like Healy. The other fork wound upward across the slowly rising plain to dead end at Lew's own sheltered ranch. For a long time Lew hesitated, but finally, coming to a decision, he took the road toward Healy's.

IV

Riding, he tried to reconstruct the layout at Healy's. There was the house, a poorly constructed, tiny one-room affair, split in two by a curtain of sewed-together burlap bags. There was a lean-to on one side of the house. There was a brush shelter near the corral. And there was the root cellar in the middle of the yard.

He tied his horse to a fence post behind the corral, having approached by a circuitous route so that the animal would leave no tracks in the yard. Then he walked through the darkness slowly, trying to stay on the high points of ground where the wind kept it scoured smooth. He had discarded the idea that Healy would cache his gold in the house. There was too much chance that Susan, a tidy housekeeper, would come upon it. He discarded the lean-to, also, and the brush shelter behind the corral. That left the cellar, empty, its door hanging ajar. The cellar was the only logical place for hiding anything.

Nervousness assailed Lew as he approached the cellar, but he fought it down. He'd have plenty of warning when Healy returned, for Healy would be sodden with drink. He went down the steps and through the door.

He struck a match on his sheepskin and stared about the moldy-smelling cellar. A rusty lantern hung from a wooden peg driven into the dirt wall, and Lew took it down and shook it tentatively. A sloshing sound told him it was partly filled with coal oil. He lifted the chimney and struck another match. He touched the match to the wick and lowered the chimney. The lantern gave off a feeble, yellow light, and Lew hung it back on the peg.

Now he turned his attention to the cellar. Its floor was littered with boxes and trash. Carefully he examined the rubbish, squinting, and, when he found finger marks in the dust on an old wooden crate, his blood began to pound. Carefully he lifted the crate and set it aside. He had gone no deeper than two inches when his hand struck part of a canvas sack. He hauled it out, knowing instantly from its weight that he had found Healy's stolen cache.

He opened the sack and peered in at the dull gold coins. Then he re-tied the sack and replaced it. He covered it carefully, and as carefully replaced the crate. He blew the lamp out and stepped out into the cold night air. Snow was drifting into the cellar's stairwell, but Lew knew his tracks would be gone in a matter of minutes. So, he hoped, would be the oily smell of the lantern that lingered in the cellar.

He climbed to level ground and headed around the corral toward the place where he had tied his horse. Hope began to stir in him, and then he heard a distant shout. He started, and quickly found his horse. He led the animal back away from the corral 100 feet. He tied him to a small clump of yucca by looping the reins around the plant close to the ground. Then he waited, his hand on the horse's muzzle, ready to stifle a whinny if the animal caught the scent of Healy's team.

The shouts grew closer, and then Lew could hear Abby crying. He scowled. Probably from the cold. Susan would be as cold as Abby, but Susan would not complain. Healy pulled up at the house, surprisingly, to let Susan and the little girl off, and the wagon made a blob of black against the snow-covered ground. Then he drove toward the corral. He unhitched his team quickly, showing Lew that he had either exercised some restraint at Solomon's tonight, or had sobered up on the way home. He turned the team loose, and then went into the corral. He caught the same bald-faced roan that Lew had borrowed nearly a year ago, and led the animal over to where his saddle lay, half covered with snow. He saddled quickly and mounted.

Excitement began to build in Lew. Swiftly he untied his horse and mounted. He followed Healy long enough to ascertain which direction he was taking, and then drew up. This was the chance Straight would have given his arm for. Lew did not know whether he wanted to take it or not. If he followed Healy, he would probably get the evidence the cowmen needed so badly. If he did not, he could return to Healy's house, could show Susan the cache of gold. He knew he could convince her that Healy was a thief. He thought that such knowledge might well release her from her blind loyalty to Abe. On the other hand, following Healy would involve him in the man's capture and subsequent death, would probably lose him Susan forever. For how could he ever explain his presence here tonight? How would he ever convince her that he was not stalking Healy for the very purpose of eliminating him so that he could have Healy's wife? He had as much as admitted to Susan that he had thought of killing Abe. She'd remember that.

He turned in his saddle and stared at the tiny, dim square of light shining through the driving snow. He could go back, perhaps could win Susan—but only at the cost of betraying Straight and Weems and Woolery, who were his friends, who had been his father's friends. Somewhere along the way every man worth his salt lays down a straight line to live by. But what good is that if he deviates from the line every time it becomes convenient?

Lew hesitated but a moment longer and then, his face strained and cold, reined around to follow Abe Healy. He was forced to spur his horse into a trot. Due to the thin snow cover, the hoofs of Healy's horse scuffed through to bare ground, leaving an easily followed trail, but Lew knew that these tracks would soon drift over, as would the tracks of the cattle Healy intended to steal tonight. There was also an excellent chance that Healy, hearing some slight sound on his back trail, might pause and bushwhack Lew. In his present mood, Lew did not particularly care what happened. If Healy ambushed him, it might even simplify matters.

After half an hour, Lew heard a shout before him, and drew his horse to a halt. Dimly in the distance, he could see the black shape of a house. A square of light showed as a door opened, and Lew could hear muffled voices. The door closed, and after a while Lew moved on, now following the tracks of two riders.

His senses sharpened with the feel of danger. An ambush now would surely mean death for Lew, might also mean that Healy would get away unhurt. He began to wonder how many men were in this with Healy. He followed the two for almost another full hour before he again heard shouts ahead and the bawl of cattle.

All this time they had been traveling due west, with but slight deviations for the contour of the land. Lew estimated that Arriola was now almost directly north of him, and that he was on Mel Woolery's MW range. Straight's place would be east of here, and Joe Weems's small spread lay along Mel Woolery's western boundary. These cattle he heard must be MW stock, but probably Healy intended to gather in whatever he found of Joe's as he crossed Weems's grass.

Lew began to wonder just what he expected to accomplish by following the rustlers. If he trailed them long enough to ascertain their destination, it would be too late for him to return to Arriola for help. Yet he knew that jumping four men was a suicidal risk that could accomplish nothing. He therefore judged that he had to know something of their plans so that he could ride for help and later intercept them. Thinking this way, he lifted the horse into a running walk, an almost silent gait, and after ten minutes raised the dim shapes of men and cattle before him.

He hoped none of them would look around. He lay over his horse's withers and clamped his hand over the animal's nostrils. Snow on the ground and snow in the air tended to deaden sound, and the noise of the cattle and their own horses made it unlikely that they would hear the sound of Lew's horse. He could hear their sour, grumpy voices complaining of the cold. He heard Abe Healy snarl: "Quit your damned belly-aching! You figger it's easier to make a livin' farmin'?"

A young voice asked: "Which way we takin' these, Abe? We going to put 'em clear through to the mines tonight?"

Abe Healy's deep, surly voice came again: "Depends on the storm, I guess. If it gits worse, we'll lay over in them red sandstone rocks 'tween the hogback an' the mountains."

Lew drew back on his reins. His horse stopped, and the

cattle and rustlers moved out of sight into the thickening storm. Lew drew the collar of sheepskin closer around his neck. His feet were beginning to turn numb from the cold. Snow lay upon his clothes, and both his hands had lost all feeling. He guessed he had as much information as a man had a right to expect. He knew their general heading, knew where they would lay over if the storm grew worse, which it seemed to be doing.

Lew took a quick bearing on the diminishing sounds of cattle and riders, then turned at right angles to this and nudged his horse's ribs with the spurs. He was not overly familiar with this range of Woolery's, yet at intervals he would sight some landmark that he knew, and adjust his course accordingly. Too, he was riding directly into the wind, and unless it shifted, this would bring him to Arriola. He hoped that Straight had not left town.

He understood that he could still back out of this, that he could still retrace his steps to Healy's homestead, with now more proof than he'd had before. He further recognized that failure to set the cowmen on Healy would establish an obligation that Susan would deeply feel. He frowned suddenly and wished he could be as unscrupulous as some men, but he continued his steady course toward town.

V

It was late when he raised the town's dim lights ahead. The Stockman's saloon was still open, but Solomon's had closed. Lew dismounted and with cold-numbed hands looped his reins around the tie rail. He brushed and stamped the snow from his clothes before entering. His face was grim and somehow regretful as he went inside.

Straight stood at the bar, his coat buttoned up, a muffler tied over his head and under his chin to protect his ears. Another five minutes and Lew knew he would have missed the man entirely. Straight was leaving. Lew came up behind him, touched his arm, and said: "I've got what we want, Phil. Where's Weems and Woolery?"

"Woolery's playing poker in the back room at Samson's store. Weems is home, I guess." There was elated excitement in Straight. He drew Lew toward the door. "How the devil did you do it? I thought you went on home."

"Never mind. I did it, and that's the important thing. Let's go get Woolery. I can pick up a pair of gloves while we're there."

They went out into the whirling snow. Straight shivered. "Devil of a night for riding." He gripped Lew's shoulder as they crossed the street. "Lew, damn you, don't be so close-mouthed. What'd you find out?"

"There's four of them. They've got a bunch of cattle and are headed west. I figure they'll lay over for the night in one of those sandstone rocks between the hogback and the mountains. That's where we've got to pick them up."

"We'll need more men."

"There's two or three of Woolery's riders in town. We can get them."

Samson's store was dark, save for a dim light that shone through the door of the back room. Lew rapped on the door. After a long interval, he heard Samson's stomping steps, and his sour-voiced: "Who's there?"

Straight said: "It's me, Phil Straight. We want to talk to Mel."

Lew heard the sounds of a padlock being withdrawn from the hasp. Then the door swung open. Mel Woolery, enormous and fat, filled the back room doorway. He boomed: "That you, Phil?"

"Yeah. Lew's got the goods on Healy, Mel. Gather up what boys you got in town and let's ride."

Samson said: "Damn you, Mel, you can't quit now. You've got all the money."

Woolery laughed. "Get even some other time." He came up the long aisle in the darkened store. The other players clustered in the back room's doorway. Lew said: "Samson, let me have a pair of gloves. I forgot mine."

Samson brought a box of gloves from a cubbyhole behind the counter and handed them to Lew. Lew set them down while he shuffled through them, looking for his size. Samson asked: "What you going to do when you catch them?"

Straight's laugh had an edge to it. "What do you think?"

Lew found his gloves, slipped them on, and moved after Straight and Woolery toward the door. Mel Woolery untied his horse and, leading him, followed Straight and Lew back toward the Stockman's. Lew and Straight waited for him outside.

After a few minutes, the fat man came back. Two of his riders were with him. Slim Hankins and Ross McFee. They untied their horses and mounted. Lew and Straight, already mounted, led out. Woolery, puffing from exertion, brought up the rear on his oversize dappled gray.

There was a certain exhilaration in the others that was absent in Lew. But it faded as the cold miles rolled behind, and once Ross McFee growled: "Why the devil couldn't they pick a decent night to steal cattle?"

Straight asked, raising his voice: "How many they got, Lew?"

"Fifteen or twenty."

They were traveling west. After two hours and a half, they raised the looming shape of the hogback ahead. They rode through the cut in the hogback where Arriola Creek tumbled through and in one sheltered spot found not only cattle and horse tracks, but a mound of dung, still steaming in the cold air.

Straight murmured: "Quiet now. They ain't over twenty minutes ahead of us."

Lew began to wonder what he himself would do when they jumped the rustlers. Perhaps it would be easier for all concerned if he lined his sights on Abe Healy. No one would know whose bullet had killed the man. He considered this for a few moments, finally shaking his head. No one would know, perhaps, but Lew himself would know.

The moon peeped through the thinning clouds, probably meaning that Healy would not pause as he had planned but would drive straight through. They turned right upon leaving the gorge, and began to rise across the arroyo-cut valley. Ahead loomed the dim and grotesque shapes of the red sandstone rocks. Lew kept his glance on the ground, following the tracks that had not drifted in so badly in this sheltered valley as they had out on the plain. Too, these tracks were fresher.

The bawl of a steer came eerily out of the drifting gloom ahead, magnified by the looming rock that was behind it, and echoed from the other rock faces across from it. A murmur of indistinct voices followed. Straight said shortly: "All right. Spread out. Don't let a damned one of 'em get away, but we want 'em alive if it's possible."

Straight fell away to the left with Ross McFee. Woolery took Slim Hankins away to the right. Lew rode straight ahead. He slipped off his right glove and took his Colt .44 from under his sheepskin. He plowed through a brush pocket and, when he came to its edge, saw them before him. They had built a small fire and were clustered about it, hunkering on the ground, their hands spread-eagled toward the fire. Beyond them the cattle bunched, moving and dispirited.

Abe Healy squatted on the far side of the fire from Lew. He was a big man, black-bearded, scowling. His tiny blue eyes, close-set above a broad, flat nose, caught the light of the fire, appearing red. Healy spat a stream of tobacco juice into the fire and the hiss of it was plainly audible to Lew.

Healy grunted, standing: "All right. Let's go."

A voice spoke somewhere to Lew's left, Straight's voice: "Wait a minute, boys." Healy halted as though frozen. Then he stooped to snatch at his rifle where it leaned against a rock. Straight's voice was immediately sharp: "Touch it, and you're a dead man!"

Healy straightened, leaving the rifle on the ground. A young voice shouted hysterically: "They'll hang us! I'll . . . !" He whirled, and flame spat from his fisted revolver. Flat and wicked came an answering shot from behind the brush screen to Lew's left. The boy let go of his gun and it fell

into the snow beside the fire. The boy's face was both surprised and sick. He fumbled at the buttons of his coat, but,
before he got it open, he folded onto the ground.

An older man knelt over him, his shoulders shaking. He
laid his face against the boy's. Lew rode out of the brush.
He could see the shadowy shapes of the others coming up
from right and left. Healy stood sullenly scowling. The
other man stood beside him, looking thoroughly frightened.
The man on the ground rose from the dead boy's side. He
had a rifle in his hands. Holding the gun at hip level, he
swung the muzzle in a tight arc.

Lew could have shot him, but the sight of the boy's
death had unnerved him. He sat his horse utterly still,
unmoving. A shot racketed from Woolery's gun on his
right, echoed almost instantly by the gun in the boy's father's hands. The rifle bullet sang away into the air, and
then the man was falling, falling down across his son's limp
body. The cattle spooked away through the brush.

Straight issued a curt command: "Slim, you and Ross go
read the brands on them cattle." He turned to Healy: "End
of the line for you. You want to write a letter to your wife?"

Woolery took down his rope and began to fasten a hangman's noose in its end. Healy did not seem to see Straight,
or Woolery. He was looking at Lew. "You're the one, ain't
you? I didn't know till tonight. Hugh said you paid my bill
with him."

Lew could feel himself flushing. He said: "If you mean
do I know a good woman when I see one, I do. She's too
good for a son-of-a-bitch like you."

Healy sneered: "But not too good to sneak around with a
cowman behind my back."

Lew could feel the flush that stained his face. He could
feel an overpowering rage. But he kept his voice quiet. "You

don't know how good a woman you got." He swung down from his saddle. He unbuttoned his coat and shrugged it off. He put his .44 in one of the side pockets and hung the coat on the saddle horn. He said flatly: "You've used your fists on her. Use them on someone who can fight back for a change."

Abe Healy showed momentary surprise, then narrowed his eyes and came forward, shoulders hunched, fists cocked. He was sure. Lew knew now why the man's nose was flat— he was probably an ex-prizefighter. But Straight put his horse between the two. He asked shortly: "Look, Lew, we're hangin' this son-of-a-bitch. Why give him . . . ?"

Lew said: "No you're not." He put his hard, level glance on Straight. "Get out of my way."

Straight mumbled some protest, but he nudged his horse forward. Abe Healy came with a rush. He outweighed Lew by a full thirty pounds, and he was hard. He had a chest like a bellows.

Lew knew a brief moment's fear. If he lost . . . if he lost this fight, he lost everything. Healy would be hung because Lew would be in no condition to prevent it. Susan would hate him for beating Abe with his fists as a prelude to the hanging. She would never understand or believe what he was trying to do.

Abe was charging, his chin tucked against his chest. His left caught Lew high on the forehead as he ducked. The right, intended for Lew's chin, smashed his lips against his teeth, and snapped his head back. Smoothly, with no wasted motion, Abe's knee came up toward Lew's groin. Lew twisted barely in time and took it on his right thigh.

He was staggered. There was no denying it. He retreated over the slippery ground. Abe, grinning, followed, mouthing obscenities that concerned his wife and Lew.

Rage leaped in Lew like a white-hot flame. His fist smashed against Abe's mouth as the man came close. His right sank in the man's kidney, again the left, cutting the craggy brow, and the right, smashing the mouth again.

Lew knew he was wasting strength, was cutting his knuckles on Abe's teeth. But he could not stand the flow of obscenity—not when it concerned and accused Susan. He was carrying the fight now, was forcing Healy back. Blood from Healy's face covered his fists, made them slick and slippery. And Healy, panting, had stopped talking, now saved his breath for the fight. He retreated until the fire was at his back, and suddenly dropped his hands.

Brief and fleeting surprise touched Lew. Was Healy quitting so soon? He said: "No, damn you. You ain't quitting yet."

But he had momentarily relaxed, and that was what Healy had played for. Abe came forward again, rushing, and his fists came up from his sides like sledges. Light rocketed through Lew's brain as the massive right connected with his jaw. His feet left the ground, and he sailed backward. He landed on his back in the snow, instinctively bringing up his knees. Abe's vicious kick caught him on the kneecap, instead of in the belly where it had been aimed.

Nausea flowed through Lew's brain, and a sort of pleasant lassitude. He felt like he wanted to laugh—because this was really funny. Abe was fighting as if he fought for life instead of death by hanging. He fought to win, and victory could only bring him the choking pressure of the hangman's noose. But Lew was fighting for a woman, for the woman he loved. His chest felt as if it had caved in when Healy's heavy sodbuster shoe landed against it. But that pain, so sharp and definite, seemed to clear his head. He rolled, felt the icy snow against his face. He came to his knees, and cocked his head to look at Healy.

The heavy shoe was drawn back again. Lew marveled that neither Straight nor Woolery had interfered in this, and suddenly he knew why. Straight would tell him afterward that they had let Abe beat him up for his own good—to keep him from making a fool of himself. He caught the kick on his shoulder, and it drove him over, rolling. But he was feeling clearer-headed now, and he forced himself to his feet.

Healy swung, missed because Lew staggered, and then the big man's body was against him, moving, driving. Lew clutched Abe's huge torso. Dimly he heard Woolery's deep shout. He knew he was beaten. But his mind would not accept it. He brought his knee up into Healy's belly. Abe grunted, and doubled over. Lew stepped away from him. He stared at the big man for just an instant, surprised that Healy looked quite as sick as he himself felt. Then his right was swinging a long, hard swing with all of his weight and the power of his shoulder behind it. He knew that if it missed his very momentum would throw him to the ground. And he knew, if it did, he would never get up. But it did not miss. With a crack like that of a bullet striking flesh, it plowed into the side of Healy's jaw. Lew heard the jaw bone snap, and then Healy was staggering backward, out, but still on his feet. A full dozen steps did he take before he collapsed into the snow, and lay staring with open eyes at the clearing sky.

It took Lew a moment to understand that he had won. He looked at Straight, still ahorseback, at Woolery's sweating, reddened, and fascinated face. Then he staggered toward his horse. The animal spooked away from him, but Lew dived to the ground and caught a trailing rein.

The drag of the rein helped him to his feet. He quieted

214

the horse with a curse, and fumbled for his coat. But he did not put it on. He got the .44 from the side pocket, and turned, cocking the hammer.

He put the muzzle on Straight. He said thickly: "You're not hanging this one."

Phil didn't say anything for a long moment. Then he said softly: "What about the other?"

Lew panted: "To hell with him!" He sat down in the snow, but the muzzle of the .44 was unwavering. He felt that he could never again get enough of this cold, sweet air. He breathed with great, long, sucking gasps. He heard Mel Woolery's and Straight's retreating voices. He heard the rustler's snarling protest.

Abe Healy sat up. His jaw hung open, slack and loose. Lew went over to him and said: "Get your horse and follow me." He walked to where the limp body of the fourth rustler swayed in the wind. Healy followed him. Woolery had lost his ruddiness, was now deathly pale. Even Straight looked sick. Lew turned to Healy.

He said: "Take a good look. If you ever come within a hundred miles of Arriola, that's what you'll look like. Now get on your horse and hightail. And don't open your filthy mouth, or I'll probably change my mind."

He watched Healy mount. He listened to the diminishing drum of hoofs. He felt utterly exhausted.

He spoke then to Straight. "There's around five thousand in gold in Healy's cellar. I know damned well his wife won't want it. I hope she won't need it. Maybe it'll repay you for part of what you've lost."

He walked over to his horse, put on his coat, and mounted. Neither Straight nor Woolery said anything, nor did they look again at the swinging corpse. Then Lew rode out.

VI

It was dawn when he rode into his home place. He turned his horse into the barn and clawed some hay out of the loft for him. He went to the pump and stuck his head and neck under its chilling stream. He filled the dipper to the brim, and took a long, cold drink. Inside the house, he found a towel, and dried his face, mopped the blood from his cut mouth.

With every muscle screaming, he changed his clothes. He looked longingly at the bed, then went out to stand uncertainly on the stoop. He began to realize what he had done. Divorce was an uncertain and long-drawn-out process, taking years sometimes. He had cut Susan and Abby loose from the tenuous support that Abe gave them. He knew he would offer financial support to Susan while she was getting her divorce, knew just as surely that she would refuse it. He even began to wonder if, when the divorce was complete, she would still want him.

He shrugged dispiritedly and walked across the yard to the barn. He saddled a fresh horse, and rode along the trail toward Healy's homestead. Last night it had all seemed so logical. Today it did not seem so. Half a dozen times Lew hesitated and almost turned back. But doggedly he kept to his course.

He struck the road half a mile from Healy's. Toward town he saw the tiny shapes of two riders approaching. He waited, and, after a few minutes, Straight and Woolery rode up. Straight said, perhaps a little sheepishly: "We got to thinking about that gold Healy had. We figured maybe he'd come back for it. We figure you went too easy on Abe, and we was damned if he was going to get that gold if we could

216

help it. It's rightly our money, Lew."

Lew's sense of depression deepened. He shrugged. "All right. Come on. Let's get this over with."

They went on and, after a few minutes, topped the slight rise and looked down into Healy's yard. Lew reined up abruptly. Two horses stood beside the house. Abe sat atop one of them, apparently arguing with Susan on the ground. Abby stood alone, gazing first at one and then the other.

Straight said—"Damn him, this time he crowded his luck too far!"—and spurred his horse down the rise, with Woolery and Lew pounding along behind. Abe whirled in startled alarm at the sound of their horses. His face was ugly with rage, and pain from the sagging jaw. His hand went after his revolver.

Straight raised his own gun. Lew yelled: "Put that up! You want to hit his wife or child?" Abe must have heard this. It must have given him the idea for the thing he did now. Nudging his horse, he rode close to Abby and, leaning down, snatched her up from the ground. He held her body against him with his left arm. His right hand held the revolver.

Straight yanked his plunging horse to a halt, and faced Abe's menacing gun uncertainly. Susan looked at Lew. Her voice was low, without spirit. "He had a sack of gold hid out in the cellar. He came back for that."

Lew looked down at her. He tried to smile. "He's been rustling cattle for two years. I kept them from hanging him because of you."

Her eyes gave him her brief thanks.

Straight said: "Abe, put the child down. Your string's played out."

The noise that rumbled in Abe's throat might have been a laugh, but for the broken jaw. His eyes were hot as they

217

looked at Lew. Lew knew Abe wanted to kill him so badly that the desire was hard to control. Abe must also know that, if he killed Lew, nothing, not even Abby could save him from Straight and Woolery. So he dropped the muzzle of his gun. He spoke over his shoulder to his wife. "Susan, get up on your horse." Then he looked back at Lew. "We're leaving . . . all three of us. I'll have Abby on my saddle until we're out of the country. Don't try to follow."

All the things Lew wanted to say to Susan were in his glance. She dropped her eyes, lifted her skirt, and prepared to mount her horse.

Abe was watching Lew, and so did not see the thing she did next. She snatched her shawl from around her neck, and flung it at the head of Abe's horse. Unused to women, to women's garb, the horse did what Susan had known he would. He shied violently, and then he reared. Abe, in an entirely instinctive gesture, released Abby and grabbed for the saddle horn. As the child fell, the horse shied away from her, and reared again.

Susan darted in and snatched Abby from the ground. The child's face was white, her eyes wide. She began to scream with fright.

Abe brought the muzzle of his gun down and struck his horse between the ears. The animal dropped to all four hoofs. Abe raised the gun, centered it loosely on Lew, and thumbed back the hammer.

A lightning thought told Lew that he was a fool. But he made no move toward his own gun. He had gone to too damned much trouble to save Abe to kill him now. Straight had no such reluctance. His gun spat wickedly. Abe swiveled his glance to Straight, showing stupid surprise, and then he slid from his horse. Susan stared at Abe on the ground for a moment. Then quickly covering Abby's face with her hand, she ran for the house.

Lew looked at Straight, who watched Abe closely, gun ready. "Phil, I'm sorry. But I couldn't kill him."

"I know you couldn't, Lew." Straight looked at Woolery. "Help me hoist him to his horse. Then let's get out of here." They left quickly.

Lew went on the house and knocked uncertainly on the door. Susan's face was white with shock as she answered it. Lew said soberly: "I led them to him, Susan. But they have been my friends as long as I can remember and he was stealing from them."

"You did what you had to do, Lew." Her expression turned soft, pitying, and somehow shy.

His heart leaped. "You don't blame me, then?"

She shook her head. "Abe had changed. He was vicious. Abby and I were both afraid of him." She tried to smile and failed. Lew opened his mouth to speak, but Susan stopped him.

"Be quiet about it, Lew. It's over. Come in and have some breakfast."

He petted Abby's smooth head awkwardly as he came into the room. He turned, and Susan was close to him. He reached out his hands toward her but suddenly stopped, and the fright subsided in Susan's eyes. She was smiling as she turned toward the sheet-iron stove.

More than anything else, Lew wanted Susan in his arms, but now was not the time for that. He sat down at the table and pulled little Abby close to him. He released a long, contented sigh. The waiting was almost over. The living was about to begin.

About the Author

Lewis B. Patten wrote more than ninety Western novels in thirty years, and three of them won Spur Awards from the Western Writers of America, and the author received the Golden Saddleman Award. Indeed, this points up the most remarkable aspect of his work: not that there is so much of it, but that so much of it is so fine. Patten was born in Denver, Colorado, and served in the U.S. Navy, 1933-1937. He was educated at the University of Denver during the war years and became an auditor for the Colorado Department of Revenue during the 1940s. It was in this period that he began contributing significantly to Western pulp magazines, fiction that was from the beginning fresh and unique and revealed Patten's lifelong concern with the sociological and psychological affects of group psychology on the frontier. He became a professional writer at the time of his first novel, *Massacre at White River* (1952). The dominant theme in much of his fiction is the notion of justice, and its opposite, injustice. In his first novel it has to do with exploitation of the Ute Indians, but as he matured as a writer he explored this theme with significant and poignant detail in small towns throughout the early West. Crimes, such as rape or lynching, are often at the center of his stories. When the values embodied in these small towns are examined closely, they are found to be wanting. Conformity is always easier than taking a stand. Yet, in Patten's view of the American West, there is usually a man or a woman who refuses to conform. Among his finest titles, always a difficult choice, are surely *Death of a Gunfighter* (1968), *A Death in Indian Wells* (1970), and *The Law at Cottonwood* (1978). No less noteworthy are his previous **Five Star Westerns**, *Tincup in the Storm Country*, *Trail to Vicksburg*, *Death Rides the Denver Stage*, *The Woman at Ox-Bow*, and *Ride the Red Trail*. His next **Five Star Western** will be *Wild Waymire*.